EVER AFTER

AN ANTHOLOGY OF RETOLD
FAIRY TALES, MYTHS AND LEGENDS

EDITED BY
RACHEL KENLEY

For more information contact:
Riverdale Avenue Books
5676 Riverdale Avenue
Riverdale, NY 10471
www.riverdaleavebooks.com

Design by www.formatting4U.com
Cover by Scott Carpenter

Digital ISBN: 9781626015401
Print ISBN: 9781626015418

First Edition, January 2020

Dedication

For Margaret Hamilton
as the Wicked Witch of the West
The first villain who ever truly scared me as a child,
And who I realized was misunderstood
once I became an adult

Table of Contents

Introduction

There is something wonderful about being wicked. And after all, what is a villain? Who gets to make that decision? And isn't the villain the hero of his or her own story? We're often as fascinated by the villain in a story as we are by the hero or heroine, and if the villain isn't strong, then the champion's journey isn't as interesting. Recent movies and books have shown the fun of what can happen when the tales we know are turned around and the villains get to take center stage. In this anthology you will find villains from fairy tale, folklore and myth. From the familiar to the fantastic. From lyrical to lascivious, and from beautiful to bawdy.

And all of them get their much-deserved happy ending.

We start with Divya Sood's original *A Lover's Tale* where a dark character finds himself at the mercy of a human, and from there move under the sea where a man ends up with a selkie spouse he didn't expect in Julie Behren's *Sea and Hearth*.

In the realm of fairytale there is more from the ocean with my story, *Part of Her World,* where the Sea Witch gets her chance to win the heart of the little mermaid. Going into the woods brings us M. Reed's

Breadcrumbs, a new take on Hansel and Gretel where those meddling kids finally get what they deserve and so does the witch. Also there is *Seeing Red,* where a red cloaked maiden finds that the wolf is more than what he seems.

From myth we see the ever-wronged Hades meet the mate of his dreams after giving her what she wanted in Susan Hawes' *Stygian Nights* (and if you ever saw the animated *Hercules,* you will particularly love this one). From the cautionary fable, we see the challenges of a deadly touch in Barbra Campbell's *Kink Midas* and in Alice Kay's emotional *Grendel's Love* we see one of literatures most horrible beasts redeemed and happy.

And speaking of beasts, no collection of fairy tales from me would be complete without a version of *Beauty and the Beast* which gets a contemporary retelling in Sara Marks' *The Prince Without A Throne.* The other contemporary retelling is Trevann Rogers' *Rumpled* where a hasty promise leads to problems and then, of course, a happy ending.

If you've ever rooted for a witch, an evil fairy or a wolf, this anthology is for you. Welcome to a world where villains win.

Enjoy,
Rachel Kenley

A Lover's Tale
By Divya Sood

I have heard that, sometimes, good things come from seemingly bad places. I never knew whether to believe or disbelieve this theory. But when I was younger and doubtful, my grandmother, whom I lovingly called Bama, relayed a story to me under the cool shade of a Peepul tree during a night with a shining moon and a few stars to pierce the sky. It was an odd story at best, but it did make me ponder the power of love and the good and bad that comes from it.

"Anshu," she said, "there are worlds we no longer know. Yet they were once. And I am about to tell you about such a world that changed a life forever. Some say it was for the better. Some say it was for worse. I want you to believe whatever it is your heart tells you."

From her words and from memory, I remember the story as well as I can now. It started perhaps as a fantasy but then aren't all stories mere fantasy until they are spun into truth? So it was with Bama's story. And here, for the first time, I share her tale.

The deewanis were a magical people who resided in an enchanted forest that has long been forgotten. Deeper than even the forest thickets, there was an introvert among them who lived in the recesses of his own mind. This was a rare quality for a deewani as they practiced communal magic. But Lokhi preferred his lonesome ways and quiet spells to their shared chants and hustle and bustle. For example, if the deewanis conjured a love spell (which they did frequently) to make two random human souls attract one another, Lokhi would not lend his wand nor his voice to the invocation ceremony. Instead, he would watch from a distance and mouth the words of the spell. When the two humans came together in love, as the rest of the deewanis cheered and toasted each other with magical potions, Lokhi would retreat into his home in the trunk of an old maple tree and smile to himself.

He was not an unhappy deewani. Rather, Lokhi was quite at peace with his ways. That is until one day it so happened there were six powerful knocks that shook his home. Lokhi traveled through his tree trunk to the bottom by the roots, and turned on the fireflies for light. As he ascended the trunk and opened the door, Lokhi stood stunned.

For there in front of him, in the soft glow of the fireflies, was no deewani but a young woman. He had never seen a human so closely, and he stared. She, in turn, had never seen a deewani before and stared back. He looked up at her, as he stood at a mere three feet, and she, although only five feet tall, towered over him. He stared at the curls of her hair as they cascaded past her shoulders and at her eyes that shone with wonder and perhaps a tinge of fear. She stared at his soft brown fur and round black eyes.

"I—" she began.

Lokhi's English was not perfect but since he loved to read in the languages of humans, he understood that she was referring to herself. He wanted to form the word to speak back but human language felt foreign in his mouth, and he couldn't make the words pass his soft pink lips and dark black whiskers.

Her lips formed words as well but it seemed she was having trouble releasing them into the thick, humid air. "I wanted...no. First, let me introduce myself." she finally said. "My name is Anjali."

"Hullo," was all Lokhi managed in a tone much gruffer than he intended.

Anjali took a step back as soon as his voice rumbled from him. "Never mind," she said and stepped back some more.

"Wait." Lokhi managed to say.

They stood for a long time, she clearly wanting to speak and ask and Lokhi not knowing what to do next. Slivers of rain started to fall from the sky, and Lokhi noticed how the water caught in the curls of her hair.

"I didn't know where to go," she said. "But then I read in *The Book of Wizardry* that only a deewani could help me. And I came all this way."

Lokhi nodded. He knew *The Book of Wizardry* well as he had written many of its chapters. The book had won accolades and been translated into 29 languages, including human languages.

"Here's the thing," she said.

Lokhi waited.

"I need a loan."

"A loan?" he repeated.

"Yes, a loan."

"We deewanis don't have any currency of any kind." He said. "So, I am afraid—"

"I have to borrow your magic."

Now in all the decades Lokhi had lived in the forest, he had never heard such a request. Not from a deewani. And certainly not from a human.

"I wish to make two souls fall in love. And I was told a deewani's magic was the only thing that could help me."

Lokhi contemplated. While it was perfectly acceptable for deewanis to cast love spells, he felt uneasy about allowing a human to do so. For one, he didn't know if a human was capable of harnessing the power of deewani magic. Secondly, he wasn't certain magic could be lent. And last of all, if he were to find a way to lend his magic, he would be vulnerable himself.

"Please," she said.

As Lokhi studied her face, he felt a warmth he had thought possible only when practicing magic. He wondered if all humans evoked such tenderness. He could have quietly shut his door. He could have declined her request. But as he stood there separated from her by a few steps and a lightly falling rain, his heart twitched with desire to help her. He wondered what was the worst that could happen if he did allow her to borrow his magic. If, of course, such a thing was possible.

"You wish to use this magic for love?"

"I wish to use this magic to find the love of my life," she stated. "I know deewani magic can draw love. I wish to have love in my life."

Lokhi considered.

"Please," she whispered again.

Lokhi caught her gaze and saw that there were tears in the corners of her eyes threatening to spill at any moment. "Let me see what I can do," he said. "Wait here."

Inside his home, Lokhi perused his bookshelf until he found *Deewani Magic and Human Interactions*. It was written in Deewani script on one side and English on the other. He took down the book and read to himself, his finger carefully following the words on the page:

"If a deewani deems it necessary to lend magic to a human, the magic must be returned within 36 hours. If the magic is not returned, it will be lost and the deewani will become human never to return to magic again.

To impart magic to a human, a deewani must hold both the human's hands in his and state, 'I lend this magic from me to you. If not returned, I know my fate and fully accept it without question.'

To return magic, the human must hold the deewani's hands and state, 'I return to you the essence of the deewanis.'"

It seemed simple enough. Lokhi replaced the book on the shelf and softly waddled to the door.

"I can lend you my magic," he stated. "But I must have it back within 36 hours."

"Yes! Yes, I will definitely return to you before then."

Lokhi took her hands in his. He felt the softness of her palms against his fur. The touch seemed to him magical in itself, and for a moment Lokhi wanted to hold her hands and not release them. He wondered if this was the beginning of what humans called "love." For although deewanis could cast love spells, they were not capable of experiencing love for themselves and no deewani ever knew what it was that he was imparting.

"What next?" she said shaking him out of his thoughts.

Lokhi carefully said the words that would lend his magic. The rain fell harder. Lightening tore the sky into two halves. Lokhi felt his magic draining from him and watched as it surged into Anjali. Finally, the transfer was complete.

"Thirty-six hours," Lokhi said.

Anjali had already turned and was running away from him.

Lokhi entered his home and shut the door. He shut the fireflies off and, in darkness, paced the floor. Minutes passed. Then hours. The sun rose in the sky and fell again into the horizon but Anjali did not return. When the sun rose again, Lokhi became restless.

At the 34th hour Lokhi's fur started to recede. In its place, he saw human skin. In the 35th hour Lokhi's face started to emerge. He looked at himself in a mirror and saw that his snout had become a nose. His face was devoid of all fur and whiskers and was the same color skin as his arms and legs. His head had only a crop of hair.

He started to panic. If he were to lose his magic, what would he do? He knew nothing of human ways and life.

With only a half hour to go, Lokhi stepped outside and looked about. The leaves were still and there was no sound. He listened for human steps but there were none to be heard.

At hour 36, Lokhi sat outside his door and felt tears in his eyes. He sat with his knees to his chest and his head in his hands. What had he done? He was now completely human with no inkling as to where to go or how to live. He could not even return inside his home as in the final moments he had grown three feet and would not fit in the tree any longer.

As he sat contemplating his foolishness, he discerned a figure in the distance. As he watched, Anjali appeared in front of him.

"What have you done?" he said. "What will happen to me now?"

Anjali knelt beside him. She slowly wiped his tears with her soft fingertips.

"I told you I wanted love," she said.

"And for that you sacrificed me? My magic?"

Anjali took his face in her palms. "My dear Lokhi. It was you I loved. I didn't forsake you. I did what I could to draw you to me. When I read *The Book of Wizardry*, I read your words and I felt as if I wanted to run to you. But I knew that as long as you were a deewani, you would never understand my heart."

Lokhi raised his head and looked into her eyes. The look she held made him keep his gaze there, without hesitation or haste. Without fear. For what he finally felt was what the humans called "love." And it was greater than any magic he could have sacrificed.

Sea and Hearth
By Julie Behrens

Tom hadn't gone out that morning with the intention of stealing a selkie pelt. If he had, he would have walked down to the ocean. That was where the selkies were, after all. Sometimes he saw one, bobbing in the water like a cork before ducking back under the waves. He knew it was a selkie and not just a seal when they waved at him or blew a raspberry, and as they disappeared, he heard the very beginning of barking laughter. They weren't usually dangerous, the selkies, but they weren't terribly polite either.

But Tom wasn't by the ocean longing for a selkie wife or a mermaid fling and a kraken death. He was in the forest, foraging for mushrooms, checking rabbit snares, looking for wild hog digs and hoping for a missed truffle. He found hardly anything that morning, so he went farther than usual. Much farther. He was out beyond the village's hunting grounds, in the wild. The sun was almost up. He was going to have a long walk home, with little to show for it.

All that morning he turned an old problem over and over in his head, worrying at it like a sore tooth. Life would be so much better with a wife. His only living child had recently married, and she no longer had time to help her father with his little scrap of the world. She had her own scraps to look after now. Three years really alone, and nine since his wife had died, and he was feeling the ache of long loneliness. He could cook and clean and forage and fix and mend and tend well enough to care for himself. Hadn't he finished raising Jess on his own? But with a wife, the winters would be warmer. The work would be lighter. He'd have someone to talk to, someone to share his little victories. He longed to be touched, and touch in return. But he had never been beautiful, even in his youth. Now there was gray in his peach-colored hair, and his eyes crinkled whether he was smiling or not. And there were so many fewer smiles. He had a small home and not much else in the world to his name. The only things to recommend him were an honest nature, most of the time, and a kind heart, but to the right person, maybe it would be enough. Couldn't that be enough?

He heard the splashing of water and laughter and his self-pitying mope was interrupted. Was he really all the way to the river? He started to turn and go home, but he then he thought there might be crayfish or freshwater shellfish this far from the human-occupied part of the river. He might even fashion himself a fishing pole of some kind. A fresh breakfast would be a welcome change. Spring wasn't quite in full swing yet, and his winter stores were down to the unsatisfying bits.

So he went to the river, and crept up on the human voices carefully. Not out of sneakiness. He had no intention of stealing. But this far out there might be bandits, or at least strangers. Tom was no innocent to violence at the hands of other men. His gentle nature painted him a target when someone wanted a target badly enough.

When he came upon the strangers, he ducked away and hid his eyes. Naked people! But he wanted to see what sort of people they were. He might have to look, to know if they were safe. He thought a quiet apology to them and looked. Then he looked some more, even as heat colored his cheeks.

It was almost all women of varying ages, bathing in the clear, cold river like it wasn't freezing. Tom was in boots and wool socks, thick pants, two shirts and a wool jumper. How were they standing the cold?

Then he saw the skins.

He took them for fish hanging from a tree at first, they were so silvery. Then his mind made sense of them, and realized they were pelts. It wasn't a long jump from that to realizing what they were. Selkies! They had come to the river far away from men to bathe in the fresh water. It made sense. One could live in saltwater only so long before it did things to one's hair and skin.

Taking a pelt would be wrong. Tom knew that. He had known a man with a selkie wife, and she was lovely and quiet and sad. She had loved their children, but when she found her pelt one day, she was gone before he came home, leaving the children behind and alone. Selkies were not human. They were not happy on land.

But Tom wasn't happy either, and maybe she would not be so unhappy after all. Maybe it was just that particular selkie, that particular husband. He could always give her the pelt back if she was so miserable that he felt sorry for her. With someone else to help, he'd have more time and energy to gather food. He could improve and expand his garden. He had a solid house and a kind heart, which is more than some could give her. Shouldn't that be enough?

And he wouldn't be so alone.

He was tempted. His conscience couldn't convince him not to. His loneliness decided for him. He reached for one skin, then paused. The slender, shining ones were probably young selkies. Wouldn't an older selkie be more likely to be happy enough? Enjoy and appreciate a little human comfort? There was a bigger pelt, not as silvery and delicate. That, he thought, would be an older selkie's pelt. He took it.

The reaction was immediate. Someone yelled, chaos struck, and the selkies scattered like startled fish. Some of them went for their pelts, and Tom ducked down behind a large tree, unwilling to look at their naked bodies just for the pleasure of seeing them. He didn't deserve that. Already the guilt was crawling over him like a swarm of insects. He wasn't a bad person, he insisted to himself. It wasn't that wrong, really, and besides, he wanted one—he wanted a selkie wife.

But it was a deeper voice than he expected that said, "Where's my pelt? Come out, thief!"

Tom hesitantly came out from behind the tree. Most of the selkies were gone. Several seals bobbed in the water to watch. An enormous naked man with a wild beard and long, matted hair stood near where the pelt had been. Tom looked down at the pelt in his hand, and realization dawned on him like a red, angry sun. Of course it was bigger and darker and coarser. It was a male's.

The selkie threw his arms up and said something in another language, but it was clearly a curse. "Great!" he said. "Now I'm married." His eyes glared daggers.

Tom approached him with the skin held out. "I'm sorry. I didn't even realize there were male selkies."

The selkie bared his teeth, and his canines were surprisingly large and sharp. He was large all over—large hands, large chest, large muscles, large... everything. Tom was intimidated.

"So you wanted a selkie wife, hmm? A pretty little thing to bear your brats and do your bidding and take your—"

"No! I thought this would be an older selkie's skin! I just—" He tried not to wring the pelt in his hands, and smoothed it instead. "I was just lonely. I didn't even think—"

"Clearly not."

Tom held the pelt out to him. "Here. Take it back." He was trying not to look at the other man's dangling bits.

The selkie laughed. "So you can come back another day and steal another pelt and another until you get one you like? Sorry, it doesn't work like that. We're married. See your hand?"

Tom looked down at his hand. There was a dark gray band around his finger. He rubbed at it. It wouldn't come off. The selkie held up his hand. There was a band on his finger too.

"But you're a man!"

"The magic doesn't care."

"But... why?" Tom said, flustered.

"Why? Never bother why. The fae laws are the way they are. That's magic that's older than you and me, older than our least remembered ancestors."

"But selkie wives run away if they get their pelts back—"

"Doesn't mean they're not still married. They can't wed again, but that's usually just fine by them, so long as they're in the ocean again. Like many women who run from a cruel husband."

"I'm sorry. I've wronged you." He felt wretched. A moment's weakness, his own greed and loneliness, had cost them both dearly. How much had he changed both their lives with this foolish action?

The selkie considered him, and his ferocious glare cooled minutely. "My name's—" And he made an unpronounceable bubbling noise. "But you can call me Bay."

"Tom."

"What's your home like, Tom?"

"It's... old, small, but it has a solid roof, strong walls, and a good well. I have a garden and a pasture, though it's laying fallow now, with no goats to run on it."

"Any children?"

"My daughter is grown and gone."

An unreadable expression passed over him that might have been grief or might have been a bad taste in his mouth. "Mine is also. We're wedded, there's no getting around that fact, so we may as well try it out, see if it'll work. Selkie wives will take off at the first opportunity, but I'm a selkie husband, and I'm quite a bit lazier. So, take me home, presumptive human."

Tom held his hands up defensively as Bay walked towards him. "I never said you could come home with me!"

Bay barked a seal-laugh. "Oh, we're past the point of you having any say in that. I'm yours now. You're obligated to keep me comfortable and fed and warm and happy. In return, I will see that you, too, are comfortable

13

and fed and warm and happy. Or is that not quite what you had in mind when you stole my pelt?"

Bay walked away and Tom followed, reluctantly. Behind him came a chorus of seal laughter, which then became human laughter, and a series of lewd and unrepeatable suggestions for how Bay and Tom might enjoy their new husbands.

* * *

Bay accepted Tom's offer of a shirt as they approached civilization, and tied it around his waist so as not to scandalize the people who lived on the outskirts of the village. He waved merrily and smiled to the perplexed people who stood up from their gardens or their work benches to stare at the mostly-naked stranger walking with Tom.

Tom led Bay to his home. It had been brighter and merrier once, but the herb and flower garden in the front had grown wild, and little things had been left unfixed for too long. The gate leaned against the fence, its hinges having rusted and fallen off. The roof was sound, he hadn't lied about that, but it sagged. Tom led the way to his door and stopped.

He turned and said, "If I'd known I was going to be bringing home a spouse, I would have cleaned up."

Bay gave him a look like an offended cat. "Well maybe you shouldn't have gone and picked one up then, huh?"

"I deserved that." He opened the door.

It wasn't so much dirty inside as... sad. His winter stores were almost gone, which meant there were no meats or herbs drying in the rafters above, giving off a sweet, delicious smell. Instead it smelled mostly of onions and potatoes, since that's what he'd eaten recently, things he had once intended to plant, rather than eat. It had been a hard winter.

The floor was stone, but it was dusty, drifting into outright dirt along the walls and in the corners. He'd given his table and chairs to his daughter and hadn't seen fit to replace them. He ate in a chair by the hearth. It was just him, after all. One room, the nursery that had held several babies then became his daughter's room when she alone survived the terrible summer sickness, was empty. The other room, his bedroom, had an old mattress of wool and feathers that lay on the floor covered in threadbare blankets and a tattered ox skin. When his old bed had broken, he'd never replaced it. The pieces still stood in the corner.

Bay spent long minutes looking around the mostly-empty little house while Tom wrung his wool hat in his hands. Finally, Bay turned to Tom and wrapped his arms around him.

Tom was a little taken aback, and didn't quite know how to respond, so he just stood stiffly while the big selkie hugged him. Then Bay said, "It's ok. I'm going to take care of things." Tom relaxed, and leaned against him, and even managed to believe him.

* * *

The first thing Bay fixed, after Tom had outfitted him in clothes that were too small, but worked well enough for today, was the bed. He sent Tom out to the yard with the washboard to wash the blanket, instructing him to get the water as hot as possible. It took a long time for the water to heat, and Tom watched, mesmerized, as Bay flung the mattress about in the backyard, yelling at it in a language Tom didn't know. He went inside, and Tom glimpsed him through the window, muscles working as he scoured the floor.

After Tom washed the blanket, hung it to dry, and shook out the pillows, he went back inside and found the bedroom clean and the mattress well fluffed. Bay looked pleased.

"I've banished the bugs," he said.

"You've what?"

"Banished the bugs. There were bugs."

"Yes I know there were bugs." They were just a fact of life, weren't they? Nothing anyone could do about it.

"I know but a few trifling magics," Bay said, slinging an arm over Tom's shoulders, "but I know how to get rid of pests. There's a cleaning fish over on the east side of the reef that taught me how."

"Thank you," Tom said, not knowing what else to say.

Bay smacked him on the ass and moved on to cleaning the main room, including yelling at both mice and bugs.

In the afternoon, Bay went to the ocean and came back with several large fish. He had Tom bake bread, more than Tom thought than they could possibly eat in the next few days. But Bay was right to do so because after supper, people began trickling by to see what in the world was going on. Tom introduced each person to his new husband, and they took this in with the flexibility common among people who lived adjacent to fairies and their kind. One day the miller may fall into a hundred year sleep, another, a frog may turn out to be a prince and on another, a neighbor may marry a selkie man. It was something they came to accept even if they found themselves smirking at this particular situation.

When the last of his neighbors left, it struck Tom that there was only one bed in the house, and he couldn't very well ask his husband to sleep on the floor or the chair. He put on his hat and muttered he was going to a neighbor's for the night.

"Oh no," Bay said, pulling him back inside. "You married me today, and you will stay with me tonight." He softened at Tom's stricken face. "You don't have to bed me tonight. We've both had a long day, but you will sleep in the same bed as I do. It's an old magic, Tom, it demands to be satisfied."

"To hells with old magic!" Tom cried, aware even as he did so that he shouldn't. "I've been humiliated today, laughed at by my neighbors who ate up my bread, had my home invaded—not that I don't appreciate all you've done," he added, coming down off his anger as fast as he'd gotten onto it. He shook his head. "I'm too tired for one more thing."

Bay tucked a knuckle under Tom's chin and raised it to look him in the eye. "Am I so terrible a beast you cannot share sleeping space with me?"

"No, of course not."

But Bay wouldn't let him look away. "I'll sleep facing away from you. I won't touch you. Until you ask me to."

Tom admitted this was as good an offer as he was going to get, and he deserved none better. He took it.

* * *

17

The next day, his neighbors brought over some clothes that might fit Bay, which delighted him. Bay continued fixing and cleaning, and Tom did his best to keep up. He fixed the leak on the chimney where it smoked, packed the drafts around the windows, and drew water from the well with ease. Tom had always dreaded working that pump. Now he didn't have to.

That evening Bay had a request for Tom: to shave off his beard, and do something more appropriate with the selkie's great mane of hair. So by the light of the hearth, Tom sat with a pot of warm water and a very sharp razor and carefully scraped off Bay's beard. He liked getting such a close look at the other man. He had a strong jaw and a lovely bow-shaped mouth that Tom tried not to think about touching. It turned out his husband was quite lovely. This was both good and bad.

Tom sat in the one chair in the house to deal with Bay's hair, and Bay sat at his feet before the hearth. He first cut out the mats that would not be combed free, and worked an oil through the rest until it could be combed. He was a decent hand at hair trimming, having had to trim his sisters', then his wife's, and then his daughter's hair for them. He left as much length as he could. It was too pretty to cut short.

He fell into a bit of a trance while he combed through Bay's hair even when it no longer needed to be combed. Eventually, he dropped the comb and just ran his fingers through it. Bay's hair was peppered gray and black, like a seal skin, and indeed, Tom could see dark spots on his scalp. Bay leaned against his legs and Tom found he enjoyed it. He was afraid to stop, to let Bay turn and look at him. He didn't want that lovely face looking up at him. He was afraid he might feel things he wasn't ready to feel.

Not that Bay cared what Tom was ready for. He hummed, and let his head fall back into Tom's lap. He smiled upside down at him. "Are you ready for bed?"

Tom touched his selkie husband's newly smooth cheek. "I don't know."

"I didn't ask if you were ready to make wild, passionate love to me. I just asked—"

"Yes I heard you."

A few beats of silence, then, "Are you, in fact, ready to make wild, passionate love to me?"

Tom smiled and shook his head. "No, I'm sorry."

"Even now that you can see that I'm a pretty catch?"

Tom let his hands splay out over Bay's broad shoulders. "I don't move that fast. I'm too old for a sprint."

Bay stood up and held his hand out to Tom. "Very well then. If we must sleep only, then we sleep. Come to bed with me."

They went to the bedroom. Bay laid down facing the wall, as far over as he could comfortably be, and Tom laid down facing the other way. He found he actually quite liked having their backs pressed together. It was warm and safe and companionable. He slept well, and long.

* * *

Tom used to feel sad as he approached his dreary little house. Now he smiled broadly at the signs of life within—a thin wisp of smoke rising from the chimney,

Bay's cheerful whistling through the open window, tuneless and ever-changing like a mockingbird song, clean cloth on the laundry line. It seemed more like a sanctuary. Home.

He noted the other changes as they came. The garden had begun to emerge through the weeds. The gate was back on the fence. The bugs remained gone, except for an enormous black and yellow garden spider on the porch, who Bay had decided should remain. The field behind the house was thick with wildflowers. While he couldn't declare Bay the cause of this phenomenon, he could at least confirm that he had begun to notice beautiful things more since the selkie descended upon his home, and who was to say that Bay wasn't responsible. Selkie magic appeared to largely consist of either nurturing something into existence or yelling at the world until it obeyed. No wonder selkies were so prized as wives.

Sometimes Bay had a look about him that Tom knew well. A far-away stare and a weight on his shoulders. At those times he left the selkie alone. He was afraid Bay would one day ask for his pelt, and then what would he do? How could he go back to being alone when he'd remembered what it was like to have... He didn't dare call it love yet. But there came an afternoon when Bay was inconsolable, and went so far as to curl up in their bed in the middle of the day. Tom sat by him and rubbed his shoulders and asked what was wrong, how could it be fixed? He hoped he hadn't guessed the answer.

Bay sat up and stared out the window. "There are some things," he said carefully, deliberately, "that are easier to bear as a seal than as a person. A seal's mind is only ever on the present, never on the past or the future."

"There are things in the past that haunt you? Or are you worried about the future?"

Bay hung his head, and asked for his pelt.

Tom's heart gave a shock. He had thought Bay was happy enough. The pelt was his to take if he wanted, but he thought he might have a little longer before the selkie gave up on him. Still, he retrieved the pelt from its place in a box on a shelf, and gave it to him, feeling sick. Please no, he thought. Please stay.

Bay threw it around his shoulders, and Tom watched as a seal's body took the place of his husband's. It was not what he was expecting. Why did Bay not go down to the ocean? Did he intend to shuffle on his stomach all the way to the water?

Also, he was enormous

He was glad Bay had rolled off the mattress first, because he would have crushed it beyond repair. Bay now took up the majority of the little room not occupied by the bed. He rolled onto his back, an impressive maneuver in one so massive, and scratched his back by wriggling against the stone floor. Tom was mesmerized by the movement of blubber under fur. Then Bay twisted to put his head in Tom's lap, and yawned. Tom slapped a hand over his mouth, to keep from either screaming or retching, he wasn't sure which. Seals had terrible, dead-fish breath, and teeth like a box of knives. Tom had once seen a bear up close and personal. The bear had nothing on the bull selkie.

Luckily, Bay fell asleep immediately, and began to snore like a crashing thunderstorm. Tom had trouble extracting himself from the room. He had to climb over part of Bay's lower half to get to the door. The selkie didn't seem to notice.

After that he didn't worry when Bay asked for his pelt. He was so happy that his husband asked him for what he needed, and it was something simple enough that Tom could give it. He wondered to himself if the selkie wives would have stayed if their husbands had given them the option to leave from the beginning.

* * *

"What's this?" Bay asked as he took a cup with dark purple liquid almost to the brim.

"Blackberry wine," Tom said. "I knew I had a bottle of it still, and I found it in the back of the closet. It's traditional on the first day of summer."

Bay took a sip, made a face, considered, then took a longer sip. They sat with their wine, sitting on the back stoop, looking out across the field. Tom chatted amiably about what the back field might be like eventually. They could get a few goats, and a donkey to drive off the predators. The donkey could pull a plow too, and then the vegetable garden might really start producing, especially with the manure they'd have to add to it. Bay listened and nodded and sipped.

Finally, Tom thought he had enough wine in him to ask, and maybe Bay had enough in him to answer. "What is it, on your dark days, that troubles you so much you wrap up in your pelt to hide from it?"

Bay hung his head. Tom found Bay's hand and interlaced their fingers. That was alright, wasn't it? Bay gave him an answering squeeze—yes, it was all right.

"I told you once my daughter was grown and gone. I didn't lie, but the way she is gone... is different from how yours is." He stopped, and Tom waited. "She was caught by a fisherman, a boat captain. They pulled her onto their boat out of the sea and stripped her pelt off her and carried her away. I didn't know what was happening until I heard her screaming. I tried to keep up, but the wind was strong that day, and far faster than I could swim."

"I'm so sorry," Tom said. "Men can be so cruel."

"They can be."

"You came with me in part to keep me from coming back and taking one of the women's pelts." Tom shook his head. "I'm sorry about that too."

Bay shrugged. "I've seen in the last months that it was rather an exception to your general nature than a ruling influence. But yes, being stronger than you, I would not be so vulnerable as the women. So I did what I could to protect them. But Tom... I want to ask you. Can you help me locate other selkies?"

"Your pod is nearby, is it not?"

"You know what I'm asking."

Tom finished his wine. "Yes, I'll try to help you find your daughter."

When they went to bed that night, Bay lay facing the wall as usual. But Tom curled up against his back, and put an arm around his waist, and Bay gave a big, huffing sigh of happiness. Tom was a little afraid that he might love his selkie husband. His beautiful, kind, generous, full-hearted, husband.

Even if he did smell too much like the ocean, like fish and seaweed and salt, on hot days.

* * *

Tom, too, found his husband more and more beautiful. The more Bay talked, the more lovely he became in Tom's eyes. Very soon, it stopped mattering so much that Bay was not human, if it had mattered at all. It stopped mattering so much that Bay was male, if it had mattered at all. But he thought the opinion of his daughter might matter, and it did.

It was a beautiful late summer day when the village and several nearby villages came together for a festival day with banners and games and food. People traded what they had too much of for what they had too little of. Tom had truffles to trade and dried herbs of every sort, which had grown in great abundance in his garden now that they were properly tended. He had fresh fish pulled from the ocean just that morning which he traded for things that would store more easily, such as apples and potatoes and hard cheese. The fishermen might have grumbled that Tom had no business dealing in fish, except that none of them wanted to get on the bad side of that husband of his, who was definitely a fisherman by way of territory, if not by trade.

Tom nervously introduced his daughter to his new husband. Jess tilted her head and looked at him curiously, then shook Bay's hand and carried on. People with fae neighbors had to be flexible.

At the end of the day, when people began to wrap up and head for their homes, exhausted and sunburnt, Jess took her father aside. They spoke quietly for a few minutes, smiled, and parted.

"What were you and Jess talking about?" Bay asked as he and Tom walked home.

Tom smiled. "She first asked to make sure I wasn't hiding your pelt. Then she said that if I didn't do my damnedest to make you happy, I was a crazy old fool, and I deserved to die alone in a bog."

Bay threw his head back and laughed. "A fine girl, and wise. You'll listen to her, won't you?"

He took Bay's hand. "Of course."

That night, he took Bay's hand again in the bedroom and sat, thinking too hard.

"What is it you're afraid of?" Bay asked softly.

"That it'll change something. That it won't be right. That one of us will be unhappy. I don't know. Something."

Bay stroked his husband's cheek with a calloused thumb. "Love isn't just sex, you know that. It's shared labor, shared hardship, shared joy, learning each other, giving. We've done alright with that so far." When Tom didn't respond, he continued. "Besides, sex isn't just one thing inserted into another, you know. It's pleasure, generous pleasure, and it doesn't ever have to be endured for the sake of someone else. Won't you let me fully be your husband, and give you joy?"

Tom raised his eyes. "You'll stop if I say so?"

"Of course."

"And... won't stop, if I say so?"

"Of course." Bay laid back on the bed, and pulled Tom on top of him to lay between his legs. His touch was electric, and his eyes held a light of excitement and vulnerability that was new.

"Oh," Tom said, and kissed him.

* * *

25

It had been nearly a year since Tom had picked up Bay's pelt when the fisherman from the next harbor over came to town. Tom was not one for staying out late with his neighbors, even when there were visitors. Most nights, he and Bay lay in each others' arms. But on this night, Tom had not come home until long after nightfall, and Bay was unhappy about it.

"Where've you been?" Bay asked, with a predator's growl in the back of his throat, fangs showing, when Tom woke him.

"I hope you won't be mad when I tell you," Tom said. "I think I've found the man you were looking for."

Bay threw back the blankets. "Tell me."

As they left the house, Bay handed his pelt to Tom and Tom shared what little he knew as they made their way to the tavern, running to keep up with Bay's considerately gentle jog. Months before, Tom had told his trusted neighbors and townspeople long ago that he was looking for others who had wed selkies. They had come and found him in his garden that evening, while Bay was fishing. Tom returned to the tavern with them and sat and listened while people questioned the visiting fisherman, talking as casually as they could about selkies. Specifically, the fisherman's selkie wife. Was she beautiful? Oh yes of course, with black hair and black eyes. How had he caught her? He was sketchy on that. When was this? Five years ago. Where? Again he demurred. Finally, Tom was sure enough. He nodded to his friends and went to fetch Bay.

When they arrived at the tavern, Tom and Bay took seats near the fisherman, and Tom brought it up to him. "Good evening to you, sir!" he said, though it was at that point more like morning, technically. "I hear you have a selkie wife!"

"People won't get off the topic of that fae tonight," he growled.

Tom bought him a drink, which softened him up a little. "I've always wanted one myself. Is there a beach where they lay their skins to dry?"

The fisherman shook his head. "You'll never find a pelt by the ocean. If they're by the ocean, they're in the ocean, pelt and all. And if they remove their pelts, well, they won't stay near the ocean with them. They'll find somewhere less obvious to put them."

"Are your children selkies? Half selkies?"

"Oh, I don't really know, my two are just wee things still. The youngest don't even talk yet."

"What's her name?" Bay said, not looking up from his untouched drink.

He hadn't been loud, but conversation around them stilled. Everyone zeroed in on the selkie bull, forgetting they were supposed to be feigning innocence. Tom stepped away from the bar, unwilling to be between them. He appreciated anew the sheer size of his husband—his broad back, his large hands, limbs like an ox. He could feel the rage radiating off him. Everyone else stepped back from Bay and the fisherman, who did not yet have sense to realize his danger.

"None of your concern," he said, foolishly.

Bay stood up, and towered over the fisherman on his stool. He was as menacing as a storm on the sea, merciless with the promise of violence in his dark eyes. He put a hand heavily on the fisherman's shoulder.

"Her name."

The fisherman tried to knock the hand away and failed. He curled his lip at Bay. "Get your hand off me, you son of—"

Bay picked the man up off his stool, kicked the stool away, and slammed him onto the bar. Glass shattered, and people shouted. Blood erupted from the man's face. Bay picked him up by his throat and held him aloft.

"*Tell me her name!*" he roared.

Two other man plowed into Bay, for all the good it did them. The fisherman wasn't completely alone, it seemed. Blows fell all around, and in the midst of the brawl, the fisherman dropped to his hands and knees and made his way out the door. Tom saw him leave and shouted for Bay.

The fisherman made it to the beach and pushed out a rowboat, rowing furiously for a ship anchored offshore. Venturing onto the water was the worst choice he could have made.

Bay paused at the shore long enough for Tom to catch up and throw him his pelt. In a second, the enormous man became an enormous seal, and surged through the incoming tide and out to deeper water.

The row boat didn't make it far before several hundred pounds of bull selkie erupted out of the water and onto the prow. It splintered apart, and began to list to the side. The man began to scream.

Tom pushed out another boat and began rowing frantically. He watched the white lines in the water in the moonlight as Bay dragged the fisherman through the waves to a small promontory point, just visible at high tide. He got close enough to see when Bay pulled the man out of the water onto the rocks. Bay hadn't completely shed the pelt. He looked like a monstrous in-between, with powerful limbs and webbed feet, a mostly human face with a hare lip, and a mouthful of carnivore teeth.

"Help me," the fisherman cried out. "Help me please!"

"Where's your home?" Tom cried out. "The selkie girl. He wants her returned!"

"Return her to me, and I will release you," Bay said. At least, that was what it sounded most like. His speech was only half human.

"Around the bay! On the far side of the shoals. A little brown house with an oak tree on either side. Wait! Don't leave me here!"

Tom gestured at Bay. "I don't think it's up to me."

* * *

While it was easy for Bay to reach his daughter by the water, it took Tom longer to travel so far, and find the house, and find the girl, empty-eyed and ragged and thin, so thin. He put her and the two children in the boat, and rowed as fast as he could to return. His body ached, screaming with exhaustion and hunger. He pushed himself to his limit and beyond. His husband needed him to do this. He had taken the selkie's pelt, and Bay had done so much for him. He could do this. He must.

It was nearing dawn on the second day when they came around the point and the rocks came into sight. Tom thought for a moment he might be hallucinating, until he saw Bay jump up and wave.

It was low tide, and much more of the rocks were

visible, but it was still surrounded by deep water. On seeing Bay, the girl showed the first sign of real life since he'd taken her out of the house. She stood, wobbled the boat dangerously, and waved frantically, calling out in that bubbling selkie language. Tom pulled her down to keep her from tipping them over.

She leaped out of the boat and into the ocean, swimming desperately to her father, as weak and small as she was. Bay pulled her into his arms as soon as she was in reach, weeping and babbling. He held his daughter and silent tears dripped down his face.

* * *

For days, she slept and slept, and Bay kept beside her. It was many weeks later before Fissure—for that was the closest translation of her name—was strong enough to be up and about. Her children were resilient, as children tend to be. They were happy to play in the garden most of the day, chasing the few bugs that remained and digging in the dirt, only venturing further when they thought they might catch the gray tabby that dozed in the sun by the road. Tom didn't have the heart to tell them they would never catch her. He kept them fed and more or less clean and put them down for naps, skills that came back to him within moments of needing them again. He made them all mattresses to sleep on in the empty bedroom, and borrowed blankets from neighbors. The house felt full again.

It took a winter and spring before Fissure felt truly strong again. Bay took her down to the sea at last, where they sat and talked and watched the water. Tom watched the children play in the surf and the rocks, keeping close tabs on them, but also listening to his husband and his step-daughter talk of lost things.

Finally, Bay picked up his pelt, and handed it to Fissure. She looked at it, uncomprehending.

"He burned yours," Bay said. "I'm giving you mine."

"Papa, you can't give me your pelt," she said softly.

"I'm giving it to you anyway."

Her small fingers tightened on it. "It won't fit me."

"It'll do well enough."

"I can't do to someone else what he did—"

But Bay pulled her into a hug. "It's mine to do with as I please, and my privilege to give it up for you. Do not deny me my choice."

"No," she said as she began to cry.

After a long time, she stood up, and draped her father's pelt over her shoulders. It was ridiculously large, but it closed around her in a loose embrace. The children stopped playing to watch.

"I'm going for a long swim," she said to them. "I'll be back one day. Be good for your grandfathers." She kissed them both, and walked to the sea. The pelt formed to her, mostly, and she dove into the waves. A moment later, a seal with a strangely slack pelt bobbed up out of the water, then disappeared.

"She'll be home soon, won't she?" the older of the two children said.

"No, not for a good while, I expect, but eventually she will return. We'll wait for her." Bay stood and picked up the smaller of his two grandchildren, and held Tom's eyes as he spoke. "Come on, my loves. Your mother has the sea, but we have a strong house, a warm hearth, good food, and love for each other. That is all we need, isn't it? Yes. Let's go home."

Breadcrumbs
By M. Reed

As I watched the human children tear around my house, an old expression came to mind: violence doesn't solve anything. It's not true. I winced as the little girl used a small cooking pot to shatter my window. A dash of violence could solve all my problems right now, but, of course, that would fly in the face of the code of hospitality, and that won't do. I dug through my cupboards, deciding I'd have to use a spell on the brats tearing up my house.

"We want candy!" the boy screamed, pounding his tiny fists on my floor.

In retrospect, it had been a terrible idea to enchant my house so that these children—Hansel and Gretel—would think it was a gingerbread house. I'd wanted to make them happy, offer them some whimsy after their parents abandoned them in the forest, but it had backfired on me in a big way. They've been eating all the sweets I could conjure for the past two days. Now I don't have a single sugary treat in the house, Hansel's throwing a fit on my floor, and Gretel is prying my house apart, convinced that if it looks like gingerbread, then it must be made of candy. In her hunt for candy, Gretel had broken most of my windows, my lantern, and ripped several cupboard doors off their hinges. Hansel had been less destructive, but much more irritating.

With a few words, I enchanted two turnips to look like ripe strawberries. "Kids, I found something sweet for you!" I felt bad for tricking Hansel and Gretel, but I couldn't let them keep destroying my house. "Look, juicy, delicious strawberries."

Gretel reached me first and snatched a radish from my hand as if I'd offered her a diamond. She popped it in her mouth without a word of thanks, then reached for the second turnip. Hansel pushed her, knocking Gretel to the ground.

"That's mine!" He took the enchanted turnip and ate it in deliberately small bites, standing over his sister, mocking her.

Gretel kicked him in the shin as she started to shrink. The shoe that kicked her brother a moment ago was left empty, her hands and feet morphing into hooves.

Hansel's eyes went wide. "Gretel?" His ears grew furry and pointed, his nose became a snout, and seconds later Hansel was the proud owner of a tail.

I surveyed the damage. Where two children once stood, there are now two little piglets snuffling around my kitchen. I rubbed my temples and realized this is the quietest my home has been since the children got here.

Because of their horrible behavior, the code of hospitality no longer applies. I would have been within my rights to banish the children from my property, but I couldn't bring myself to send them back into the forest. Instead, I herded them outside to my chicken coop.

"I'll bring you food and water here every day," I said, arranging some old towels in the coop so they would have somewhere clean to sleep. "There's no fence, so you're free to wander, but if you stray too far outside my property something might make a meal of you." The piglets stared at me in, I assume, terror. Their preternaturally keen eyes were fixed on me, unblinking. "And if you wreck anything else while you're here, I'll eat you myself." I grinned at the absurdity of what I'd just said, but my words seemed to have left an impression on the piglets. They backed into a corner of the coop, watching me all the while. Rather than reassure them, I turned on my heel, deciding that frightened, well-behaved child-pigs were preferable to the screaming monsters I'd been dealing with for the past two days.

Once the children were settled in, I started cleaning. I started by going from room to room, sweeping up stray glass. By the time I was finished, I could still feel the breeze through the remnants of my windows, but I was no longer in danger of cutting myself as I moved around my house. I was angrily trying to reattach one of the cupboard doors when I heard a flock of birds startle and take flight. Squinting, I saw two humans on horseback enter the clearing near the creek.

I stood, arms crossed, on my porch knowing the only reason humans would enter my clearing is if they wanted to see me. The forest can be dangerous, and I'm the only one who lives out here. Occasionally, someone will get lost and stumble onto my cottage, as Hansel and Gretel did, or they'll come here to try to strike a bargain with me, but no one comes to socialize.

"Good afternoon, witch," the man greeted me, swinging down from his saddle. He'd added a little extra venom to his voice when he referred to me as a witch, and I could tell by the lines etched on his face that he wasn't happy to be here.

"You can call me Nia," I corrected him, hoping he wouldn't insist on calling me a witch. I forced myself to uncross my arms and try to look welcoming. "Can I offer you a cup of tea?"

The man glowered at me from under the brim of his hat. "We don't have time for that. We're here for the children. Return them now, unharmed, or we'll take 'em by force."

"Children? What children?" I asked playing dumb. Strictly speaking, I'm not a witch, as the man imagines. I'm a faerie. It's an understandable, though annoying, mistake since I do possess some magical talents, but, unlike a witch, I can't lie. I thought for a second, choosing my words carefully, then spread my arms and gestured around the clearing. "There aren't any children here. Just the pigs, chickens, and ourselves." Not technically a lie. "You don't mean to tell me that there are lost children wandering around in the forest, do you?" A misdirection.

The man took an aggressive step toward me before his companion stopped him.

"Actually," the woman interrupted, her hand holding the man's sleeve to keep him from doing something foolish. "I think what Carl was trying to say is that we think the children might have been on their way here, and we were hoping you'd seen them."

"Why would they have wanted to come here?" I asked.

The woman released Carl's sleeve. "The children—Hansel and Gretel—told their friends they heard their parents talking about leaving them in the forest. Then, they started asking people in Miding if any of them knew where you lived." The woman raked

35

her fingers through her hair nervously. "It seems Hansel and Gretel believed that you're a witch and that you might be able to grant wishes for them."

Carl's beady eyes gleamed dangerously. "But the kids got the story wrong, didn't they? You don't do magic for free." He took another step toward me, wagging his finger as he spoke. "You exchange your spells for fat little children to eat. Admit it!"

"I don't eat children," I answered flatly, my last empty threat to Hansel and Gretel flashing to mind.

He looked like he was going to hit me. I wanted Carl to hit me. As soon as he tried to hurt me, he would no longer be under the protection of the code of hospitality. Everything about him, from his accusatory tone to his taste in hats, irked me, and I wouldn't mind showing him exactly how wicked and powerful I can be.

The woman stepped between us. "Alright, Carl, you can go now. I can find my own way back."

"You can't stay here alone!"

"I was sent to inquire about the kids," she said. The woman was young and surprisingly composed in the face of her large, angry companion. "I allowed you to escort me here, but if you're going to act like this, you can go back to Miding and wait for me there."

Carl glanced back and forth between us. "Fine," he said, swinging onto his horse. "But you'd better bring those kids with you, or I'll be making another trip out here to visit your witch friend." He drew a finger across his throat. "And I won't be coming back alone." Carl kicked his horse into motion and disappeared unceremoniously from the clearing.

"So," I said, after a long, awkward pause. "Can I offer you something to drink?"

* * *

"Do you have sugar?" Amy asked, stirring her tea.

I privately cursed Hansel and Gretel. "Sorry, fresh out." I sat, pouring myself a cup. "So, why does Carl think I eat children?"

She rolled her eyes. "William, the blacksmith in Miding, swears you took his daughter in the night and ate her."

I sipped my tea to hide a smile. "Isn't Carl a little old to believe nonsense like that?"

I knew exactly what had happened. William did make a deal with me. After his wife passed, he felt trapped by the obligation of raising his daughter alone. Hurting financially, William asked if I would take his daughter in exchange for enough gold to open a forge. Since part of my job is to strike bargains with humans in exchange for their servitude, I gave William his gold and sent his daughter away to work for a faerie family in the night lands. Apparently, after she was gone, William decided to cast me as the villain of his story to the people of Miding. It was a clever ruse since no one would believe my word over his. The human capacity to lie never fails to impress me.

Amy set down her tea. "Carl isn't the only one who thinks you're a witch."

My heart sank. I'd hoped Amy wasn't so soft-headed as to believe random gossip. I tried not to look disappointed. "You think I'm a witch, too?"

"No." She took another sip of tea, never breaking eye contact with me, blue eyes boring into me. "Not a witch."

I tried not to let my eyes go wide. "Oh," I laughed. "What do you think I am?"

Amy smiled. "We've met before. Do you remember?"

Changing the topic, speaking in vagaries, it was an almost fae-like response. I studied her. Fae creatures are a diverse group, but they're nearly always tall and thin with pointed ears. Amy was short, curvaceous, and her ears looked entirely human. However, her coloring reminded me of someone.

Before Miding was formed, there was just one human who dared to live in the forest, Stephen Seiler. I'd tried to make a deal with the old trapper to convince him to leave, but no matter what I'd offered him, he turned me down. After his red-brown hair had gone gray and his blue eyes had clouded over with blindness, his family moved here to take care of him. I'd gone to visit him only once after his family came. Stephen had always been kind to me, so I'd decided to restore his sight, free of charge. I wanted him to spend his remaining days able to see his granddaughter grow. He'd introduced us.

"You're Amelia Seiler." I shifted uncomfortably. I'd told her grandfather too much. Now I needed to find out what he'd told Amelia.

"That's right," she said. "And that's how I know you aren't a witch. You're a faerie, aren't you?"

I couldn't lie, but I couldn't tell Amy the truth, either.

She reached across the table and wrapped one of her hands around mine. "You were kind to my grandfather. I don't think you're evil, but my grandpa told me to be careful around faeries, and I doubt you're telling me the whole truth."

Amy had as good as told me that she knows I'm a liar, but she'd done it in a caring, non-judgmental way. Heat raced up my arm, radiating from her fingertips. She was the first person to make me feel vulnerable in a long time. I loved it. I hated it. I needed to do something to break away from the intensity of her stare.

I disentangled my hand from hers. "Alright, I'm a faerie," I admitted. "Why would I hide the children? Do you think faeries eat people?"

She crossed her arms and drew a haughty smile across her face. "Quit playing games. You know as well as I do that you'd never eat anyone." Amy rolled her eyes at me, still wearing the same arrogant grin.

"That's not true." I leaned forward. "I'm thinking about eating you right now."

That did the trick. Amy's face flushed redder than her hair. Humans, for whatever reason, always seem to be attracted to faeries, and from the way Amy's eyes fought to avoid looking at me, she was no exception.

The only problem is that I feel drawn to her as well.

I can't say why. Amy's no great beauty, she's just another soft, squat human, but something about her made me want to know what it would be like to touch her, hold her. Maybe, it's because her knowledge exposed me in a way I've never been before. Because being around her made me feel a dangerous rush. No matter the reason, Amy seemed like fun, so I decided to play with her.

"I'll make you a deal," I said before she could recover from my comment. "Hansel and Gretel are here on my property, but you'll never find them. I'm so sure of it that I'll let you search all day tomorrow—from sunrise to sunset—and if you do find them, I'll not only let you leave with them, but I'll grant you one wish of your very own."

Amy raised an eyebrow. "And if I can't find them by sunset?"

"If you can't find them, I'll fetch them for you myself, and you'll be allowed to return them to their parents, but after that, you'll owe me a favor." I couldn't help but grin menacingly at her.

"What favor?" She asked skeptically.

"I haven't decided yet," I said examining my nails.

"But, you'll still let me take Hansel and Gretel back to Miding?"

I nodded. "That part is non-negotiable. They're quite irritating." A laugh exploded out of her, and I couldn't help but laugh along.

"So, if you somehow find Hansel and Gretel, what are you going to wish for?" I asked, a little afraid of the answer.

"I haven't decided yet," she said with a crooked smile.

"You're lying."

"I am!" She looked so proud of herself. "Now, I've got to get some sleep. I have children to hunt tomorrow."

I let Amy sleep in my bed. I laid awake on my couch most of the night, thinking about her, and about what favor I wanted to ask of her.

* * *

40

Amy started her morning by searching my embarrassingly messy home for Hansel and Gretel. My cottage is small and plain. I've got a living room, kitchen, bedroom, bathroom, cellar and a mudroom. Amy could have searched every nook and cranny of my house in just a few hours, but she didn't check any of the obvious places where children could hide. She moved quickly between rooms, surveying her surroundings and moving on.

"You don't seem to be looking very carefully." I stretched, teetering on the threshold between my bedroom and kitchen, bracing myself against the doorframe. "Maybe you're more interested in owing me a favor than you want to admit."

"I don't plan on owing you anything." She reached deep into her satchel, a thin smile on her face, and pulled a tarnished silver ring from her bag.

I recognized the ring. It was from my own jewelry box, but I hadn't seen it in decades. The ring allows the wearer to see through faerie enchantments. "Where did you get that?" I asked, shifting uncomfortably in the doorway.

"My grandfather was never a rich man. He stole this during one of his first visits to your cabin. It was why he never wanted to make a deal with you. He knew what you were from the start." She slipped the ring on her finger and looked around the room, eyes settling on me.

The glamour that made me look human is no match for a faerie ring of true sight. I did my best to cover my ears with my hands. Some faeries are lucky, they have wings that can be tucked away or tails that can be hidden in their clothes, their ears form subtle

41

points that can be hidden away with the right haircut, but there's no way to make me look human without magic. For a start, I don't have the long, black hair that humans see because of my glamour. My hair is short, blue, and unmistakably inhuman. Worse, it wasn't my biggest problem. I have two nubby little horns, slitted pupils, and a pair of huge, deer-like ears.

Amy looked confused. "That's all?" She gestured around the room. "Nothing here is enchanted." Without much in the way of magical items for her to ogle at, Amy stepped close to inspect me. "The only thing you're trying to hide is yourself."

I lowered my hands, my pathetic attempt at hiding my ears wasn't working anyway. Amy stepped so close to me I could feel the heat radiating off her body. She stood on her toes and reached up to touch my horns. I studied her face, looking for any sign of fear, but all I could see was curiosity. Amy shifted her focus from my horns to my ears, gently running her fingers along them. It tickled, and one of my ears flicked away from her touch. She giggled and jerked her hand away.

While Amy had been inspecting me, I'd been studying her. Curiosity, intelligence, tenacity, and a soft, warm body. I wrapped one arm around her waist and pulled her into the doorway, pinning her against the doorframe. I felt her stiffen with fear. From what I've seen, Amy knew enough about faeries to be frightened of me, but she didn't pull away. I leaned down to match her eye-level, giving her a good look at my vertical pupils.

She crushed her mouth against mine. The kiss was rushed, sloppy and electric. Her breasts pressed against my own almost non-existent chest. I could feel her heart fluttering wildly against her ribcage, like an animal caught in a snare. I kissed back, matching Amy's intensity, parting her lips with my tongue.

Amy pulled back. "Nia," she panted. "What are we doing?"

With one finger under her chin, I tilted her head up and to the side, so I could whisper in her ear. "You came to my cabin with a ring of true sight. I can only assume that you brought it here hoping to see some faerie magic." I could feel Amy quaking. I planted a light, slow kiss on her neck. "The way I see it, we have two options. We could stop what we're doing and start looking for the brats again, or we could step into my bedroom, and I can show you what you've been wanting to see." When I stepped back to see Amy's reaction, I realized I'd been holding her wrist the entire time. There were white marks where I'd held her too tightly. We'd both been too caught up in one another to notice.

She took my hand and led me into my bedroom. Even though I know we're alone in the woods, I swung the door shut behind us, determined that we not be disturbed.

* * *

Amy slept in the crook of my arm, breathing lightly. I've never felt comfortable around humans. When Miding was founded, I considered moving deeper into the forest, but now I wondered if some humans weren't so bad. I brushed a stray strand of hair away from her face, and she stirred.

"Hello," she said, smiling up at me. Her eyes opened wide. "What time is it?" she asked, sitting up in bed.

Without waiting for an answer, Amy jumped up and frantically started pulling on her breeches. She glanced out the window as she put on her shirt. "Sunset." Amy was dressed, but the frenetic energy that possessed her a moment ago ebbed away. "It's already sunset. I lost."

"Well," I said with a wink. "I guess now you owe me a favor."

I'd meant it as a joke, but Amy looked at me in horror. "Did you plan this?" she asked, gesturing to the bed.

"Of course not!"

Amy held up a hand to silence me. "Just show me where Hansel and Gretel are hidden."

I could feel the rage emanating off Amy as I led her to my chicken coop. The piglets had already settled down for the night on their impromptu bed. With a wave of my hand, the pigs morphed back into children. They rushed over to Amy and threw their arms around her legs.

"We were so scared!" Hansel cried, burying his face in Amy's shirt.

Gretel pointed at me. "She said she was going to eat us!"

Amy glared daggers at me. "Well, you two don't have to worry about that. I'm taking you home." She practically dragged the children from the chicken coop and back to where her horse was grazing.

"Amy, wait-"

"Not now, Nia," Amy said, cutting me off with another glare. "You'll get your favor after I take Hansel and Gretel home."

I didn't know what to say or do, except watch the three of them vanish into the forest.

* * *

I tried not to think about Amy, but I couldn't get her out of my head. I missed having someone to talk to, someone who wasn't afraid to challenge me. I couldn't help but replay how it felt to have my hands running over her body, how we'd kissed and then how she'd stormed off with those little brats. Every word she'd said ran through my head on repeat.

It took two days for Amy to reappear on my property. Once again, I put on a pot of tea and went to greet her. When she'd first arrived, I was concerned that I wouldn't like her. Now I'm worried she doesn't like me.

Amy swung herself off her horse and faced me. "So, have you decided what you want from me?"

I had thought about what favor I wished to ask of Amy. I'd thought about asking her to drink a love potion or to wear a charm so she wouldn't remember our fight, but I couldn't bring myself to ask something like that. I knew if I tried to enchant Amy into liking me again, I'd always wonder if that was the only reason she stayed. I also thought about making her swear not to tell the villagers in Miding about me, but Amy didn't seem like the sort of person to share someone else's secrets.

"I have," I said finally

"And," Amy prompted me, impatient to be done with me.

"I want you to talk to me," I began, wondering if I was wasting my favor on such a simple request. "I want to have an honest conversation with you about what happened between us."

She looked wary. "Is that all?" Amy crossed her arms protectively over her chest.

I nodded. "After we're done talking, if you're still mad at me, you can leave, and you won't owe me anything."

"Fine," she said. Amy dropped her horse's reins so it could graze and strode past me toward my own house. "Let's get this over with."

I hurried after her, but by the time I entered my own home, Amy was already seated at my kitchen table, tapping her foot impatiently. I poured her a cup of tea, and her eyes widened ever so slightly.

"Don't worry," I said, pouring a cup for myself. "Enchanting a well-behaved guest without their permission goes against the code of hospitality."

She glared at me. "You turned Hansel and Gretel into pigs."

"They broke all of my windows!" I gestured to the empty window frames along the exterior wall of my kitchen.

"They're children," she reminded me sharply. "This is a waste of time." Amy drained her tea and stood. "Is there anything else?"

Sensing that I was running out of time, I asked the one question I really wanted an answer to. "Do you hate me?"

She paused, still standing over the table. "No, I don't hate you."

My heart rose into my throat.

"I like you more than I want to," she said, unable to meet my eyes. "But I don't trust you."

"Isn't there anything I can do to make you trust me?"

She shook her head. "That's not how it works. Trust takes time, effort. You can't just cast a spell and make me trust you. Not if you want this to be real."

"If you'd found Hansel and Gretel, what would you have asked me for?"

"I didn't find them, so it doesn't matter."

"It does," I insisted. "Please, tell me." I reached across the table and took her hand, hoping she wouldn't pull away.

"I was going to ask you to make me into a faerie." Amy blushed. "You're powerful, immortal, interesting. I'd give anything to be like you."

"What if we make a new deal?" I asked, standing so I could look her in the eyes. "I'll make you a faerie, and you stay here with me."

She sighed dramatically. "I can't commit to staying with someone I don't trust!"

"Not forever," I said, yielding some of my power. "You'll stay here, with me, for one decade or until I dismiss you. If I can't prove to you that I'm trustworthy, and make you fall in love with me in that time, you'll be free to go. In exchange, I'll turn you into a faerie."

She walked carefully around the table to stand next to me. I froze, frightened that if I moved I might scare her away. Amy stretched herself up and kissed my cheek. I felt warm and couldn't move. I couldn't even make myself breathe.

"I think, I might already love you," she said, casting her eyes to the floor. "Apparently that can happen before trust. Or perhaps I trust you more than I think."

"Does that mean we have a deal?" I asked, slowly recovering from the unexpected kiss.

"Yes." She nodded, closing her eyes. "Make me a faerie."

I crossed the room and pulled a knife from a drawer, the noise prompting Amy to open her eyes.

She looked afraid as I approached her with the blade, but she didn't try to flee. I wrapped my hand around the knife, pulling it quickly through my grip, leaving a trail of blood and pain in its wake. I forced myself not to wince, trying not to frighten Amy. I wiped the knife on my pants and took Amy's hand, gently drawing the blade across her palm. I clasped her injured hand in my own, letting my blood flow into her veins until I saw the transformation begin.

Even I wasn't sure what to expect. Faeries take on so many different physical forms I couldn't predict what Amy would look like once she'd turned. Her ears grew in first, pointed and fox-like, blending naturally with her red-brown hair. Next came a bushy tail, to match the hair and ears. Her body slimmed, making her look more faerie-like, but her breasts remained the same size, and she didn't grow any taller. Her teeth became pointed, and her nails grew long. Her pupils stayed round, unlike mine, but her irises turned an unnatural red.

"I need a mirror," Amy said once the transformation seemed to be over. I guided her to the bathroom, and she drank in her changed body. She pulled at her now loose clothes, touched her new ears, and twitched her tail. When she was done, Amy turned to me, red eyes flashing. "I look beautiful!" She grinned at me with pointed teeth.

I cupped her cheek in my hand. "You always looked beautiful to me."

Amy beckoned me wordlessly out of the bathroom, practically skipping. I smiled when I realized she was bringing me to the bedroom.

"Come," she urged me, pulling at my hand. Amy winked at me. "I want to try out my new body."

The Prince Without A Throne
By Sara Marks

I chose to be here.
I chose to be here.
I chose to be here.

I've been chanting this to myself while I sit in this...
my room. I chose to be here. My being here keeps my
father and sisters safe. My being here gives the rest of
them a better chance to survive. My father is needed,
and I am not.

    The room reflects the entire estate—ravaged. I
have vague memories, from my childhood, of the
grounds lush and green and the gardens blooming with
flowers through spring and summer. I remember a
field full of Black-eyed Susans, Hydrangeas lining a
walkway, and rose bushes so abundant that the smell
of them wafted down the street. When I smell a rose, I
think of summer walking through these gardens. The
family who had lived here were descended from
deposed Russian royals. They opened the estate in the
summer so the town's residents could wander through
the gardens and greenhouses. People, like my mother,
would buy clippings for their yards hoping to have
their own piece of this beauty in their homes. It was

beautiful, even into the fall when it all died for a few months.

They had one son, Nicholas, but they called him Nicky. The town called him the Prince Without A Throne. He was the town bully, isolated him from the other children for too many years. I was younger than him, but my sisters always complained how he would pull their hair, jump out of the bushes at them, rip roses out of their hands, and run wild through the gardens. His nanny was always chasing after him until she was fired. She sued for wrongful termination, and it took over a decade to go through the court system before she lost. The nanny claimed the family lied and accused her of things she hadn't done. She promised they would pay. The town gossip started to spread then: the nanny was a witch, a sorceress, the family's Rasputin, and she would curse them with her magic.

The family left town, shut down the estate, put up a gate, and the house fell apart. Each year the gardens got wilder the vines wove through the fencing and gates, obscuring any view of the house. The sickness of the house trickled into the town over the next 20 years. My own family was infected when my mother died from pancreatic cancer when I was 15, the youngest of her three girls. My older sisters were both in college by then. A year later, my father's business closed. Dying slowly is expensive, and my mother's death had felt like an eternity. We were left with nothing and had to move into a small apartment downtown. I had to work a part-time job to help make ends meet and, after I graduated from high school, could only go to college online. Even though I got grants and scholarships, I needed to be at home to help make ends meet. My sisters weren't as lucky; they both had to drop out before graduation, move home, and get any job they could to help pay for the basics in our lives. Once they returned, all three of us shared one bedroom.

I lost track of time as I thought about my situation and did the math. I had been five when the nanny had filed her lawsuit, 15 when it had ended, and now 25. Nicky was five years older than me; 10 when his nanny was fired, 20 when he won the lawsuit, and would now be 30 years old. That beast who had locked me in this room was too young to be anyone but the Prince Without A Throne. Not that I would consider that monster a prince.

"Welcome," voices whispered in my ear.

I looked around and saw nobody else, but the room had changed as the sun had set. When he put me in here the wallpaper had hung in strips, the wood floor was dull, furniture had been scattered around the room in various stages of disrepair, and the fabrics were all tattered. Now the wallpaper was rolling back into place by some unseen magic. I got off the mattress and walked to the wall by the door, intently watching the strips of wallpaper move up the wall and glue themselves back into place. When it was finished, the color bloomed, spreading from the tiny white flowers on the field of blue. I touched a flower, almost as if I expected to be able to scatter the pollen or have the magic spread to me, but all I could feel was the hard wall as if nothing had ever been wrong with the room.

I turned when I heard the sounds of the furniture hitting the wood as it was uprighted and put itself back in place. The bed had been rebuilt with clean linens and fluffy pillows. The curtains fluttered back to life, and the crisp crease folds and bright blue fabric framed a clean and closed window. It took no more than a minute for the magic to spread the room and wake it up. It ended, as if an encore, with the closet door swinging open and dresser draws sliding out to reveal clothes I that were obviously for me. The fabrics were silks, linens, and soft cottons. Clean and expensive, as if for a modern princess. Even the underclothes were luxurious and perfectly fitted to me.

I found a simple silk blue dress on the bed when I turned back to it. It was the same cornflower blue as this room and one of my father's favorite colors because it made my dark brown eyes shine. Was the magic of this house reading my memories?

"Please join him for dinner," the whispers said again.

The door remained locked when I tried the handle. I sat on an armchair, now clean and beautifully upholstered to match the room. I didn't want to wear the dress and, even though I was hungry, I refused to change out of my jeans and T-shirt, too frustrated and tired to put forth any effort. I had been fired from work, after the announcement that a unionization attempt at the store meant they had to let us all go which meant one less income. Then my father told me about sneaking on to the estate, stealing the last rose on a bush, and the beast who threatened to kill him unless he sent a daughter in exchange for the rose. The claw marks on his arms convinced me to leave right away.

I sat there as the light faded outside and lamps in the room turned on. The magic offered me more items for the dress: a necklace, beautiful shoes, a soft scarf but I refused to move.

"Let me out," I said to nobody.

The lock clicked, and the door swung open to a lit hallway. Had I won a battle? Who had lost? The beast or the magic?

The dining room was easy to find as I followed the path of repairs. Rooms remained dark as I passed them, and I wondered what I would find inside. The smell of food got stronger as I walked, and my path ended in a formal dining room. It was already rebuilt and cleaned but empty. I didn't see any food or, thankfully, any company. A chair pulled away from the table and, as I sat down, my place setting appeared just before serving pieces full of food. I could smell roasted chicken and sweet potatoes. I reached to serve myself, but the magic lifted each piece and put it on my plate. It seemed to know how much I wanted. When my plate was full, the white wine filled one glass and a decanter poured water in the other. I wasn't sure which of the forks to use, staring at them until one wiggled slightly.

I thought I would eat alone until I heard the heavy footsteps of my host. I felt my heart race as the steps got louder. He crashed into the room, knocked over his chair, picked up his plate, and shoveled food into his mouth. I swallowed what I had been eating and tried to avoid moving until he left again. I couldn't help but stare at him the entire time, eyes wide and taking in every detail.

The boy I barely remembered had jet black hair and dark brown eyes. This beast reminded me of a lion, his mane wild, rich auburn in knots covering his head and his face like a beard. I could see bits of food in the mess of tangled hair. His skin was covered in short light brown hairs, much like the lion he resembled. I could barely see his eyes through the mess of his mane, but what I did see looked amber and more human than I expected. His face was distinctly human. His nose straight with the flare of a Roman statue and his lips thin. When he dropped the plate, almost breaking it, he turned to leave, and I saw a straight, low tail with a tuft of hair at the end.

"He's very sorry," the whispers said.

* * *

I only saw the Beast at meals for the first month I lived in the house. He refused to talk to me, look at me, or even acknowledge my presence. Fortunately, the house and the magic sustaining us seemed to bend to my will, offering me entertainment. I explored the library, pulling books to read, and found more by my bedside each night. It would even return the others to the library when I was done. Each room I entered offered something new, but if I ignored the offering, it would select something new the next day. The only thing missing were electronic items. Even my phone, one of the few things I had brought with me, ceased working on the property.

I avoided Nicky's quarters, the hallways remaining dark. I talked to myself, the magic only whispering instructions and apologies to me when necessary. Winter started after the first month, and the snows kept me inside, nobody maintaining the grounds. I found winter clothes in my closet and heavy coats in a mudroom in the back of the house. I put them on but didn't get far as the snow got higher with each storm.

There was another library next to the dining room. I was sure the room was where the men would, once upon a time, go to drink and talk after dinner. Now it was a dark room that smelled like furniture polish and was filled with books. It was different than the library by my room, but there was a fireplace which came alive every time I entered. I would sit in a soft leather armchair, a blanket over my legs, hot tea to drink, and read every night.

It was in this room that things changed. It began the same as every other night. Nicky stomped into the dining room, knocked over his chair, ate while standing, and then stomped away, ignored me. When I finished, I got up and went to the other library. I was comfortably reading by the fire, warm under my blanket until the pounding of larger feet came down the hallway. I sat up, freezing as Nicky staggered in, his eyes focused on the fire before he walked over and lay down next to it, grabbing a pillow off a chair as he passed it. He closed his eyes and fell asleep instantly.

This gave me the chance to see more of him. He was wearing tattered pants and a ripped sweater, his feet bare. His hands and feet were still human, like his face. His arms were exposed, the sleeves of his sweater torn to shreds. Did he have claws? I didn't see any, but his fingernails looked manicured to resemble them. I was curious about the rest of his body but too afraid to more, let alone try to expose more of him. He was lean and muscular, from what I could tell, as if he prowled around his own quarters chasing mice. If his hair hadn't been so mangy and gross, I could imagine running my fingers through it and scratching behind his ears. I was disgusted with myself, remembering he was a monster and would probably kill me before he allowed me to do that.

I moved slightly, trying to escape the room, and he was quickly on his feet lunging at me—staring into my eyes. I watched his nostrils flare, and he leaned over me, hand gripping the arms of the chair. I saw his thumbnails extend and realized these were his claws. I cowered in the chair as he smelled me.

"You're still alive?" He asked in a low growl.

He smelled like he hadn't showered in years and I couldn't hide my disgust even though I turned my face away.

"Yes," I whispered.

"I shouldn't be surprised. The house doesn't allow anything to die," he said as he stood up and sauntered out of the room, his tail still low and straight but also slowly waving as if to entice me.

I ran to my room and threw up everything I had eaten at dinner. I came out of my bathroom, always sparking and clean, to find a plate of shortbread cookies and tea waiting for me. Was the house apologizing?

* * *

The house seems preoccupied the next morning. I woke up late, found no new book waiting for me, and sat at an empty table before going into the kitchen to make my own breakfast. I was afraid it was now ready to let me die as if Nicky had turned off the magic. I went directly to the kitchen at dinner, expecting to make my own but couldn't get in. I tried through the dining room, but that door was locked as well. I turned back to the table and saw two place settings next to each other. I knew what that meant and braced myself for the smell and hoped he would eat as quickly as he always did.

The beast who entered the room was transformed. Not only could I smell the soap he had used to bathe and the scent of roses from the shampoo that had washed his hair, but his clothes seemed new. Nicky's mane had been trimmed and cleaned, the beard hair slightly thicker than the hair on his face and I could now see how the auburn hair went down his neck and under his collar. He wore a white shirt, the top two buttons open to reveal his collar bone and some of his chest. The light brown hair on his face traveled down his neck and on to his chest, getting thinner and sparser. For a brief moment, I wondered how low it went, my eyes moving down his body and stopping at his belt. I pursed my lips and bit them inside my mouth, trying to avoid any sounds, but he stared straight into my eyes, looking at me like I was his prey. I felt my teeth release my lips, and I narrowed my eyes.

"Sit," I said to him. I was nobody's prey.

His eyes went wide, and his body obeyed without a word.

I sat next to him, and the food began plating as soon as I put my napkin on my lap.

I refused to acknowledge him, other than to correct his behavior. He had made an effort to look presentable, but I was going to make him behave as civilized as he looked.

"Use the fork," I told him when he picked up a piece of the brisket with his fingers.

I didn't look at him but could see him, in the corner of my eye, staring at me, mouth agape. He obeyed this instruction too, and every other one I gave him through dinner.

"I remember you," he said when his plate was empty, his voice a deep rumble that made me shiver a little like he had blown on the back of my neck. "You used to come with your bitchy sisters. They would rip the roses off the bushes and scatter the petals around the grounds of the estate. My mother would cry when she saw them."

I didn't respond, not able to remember what my sisters did when we once visited the gardens.

"You," he continued, "always patiently waited for someone to come with the garden sheers and you carefully picked the one you wanted. It was always from the bright pink ones my mother had created herself."

"Yes, I remember those roses," I said, remembering how I always tried to pick one that was perfectly bloomed because I didn't want to ruin the beauty of new buds.

"Your sisters were like everyone else, entitled to my mother's hard work and taking it to make their own. You all came without invitation, took what you wanted, and sometimes offered something in exchange."

"And you bullied them for it?" I asked, angry at his criticism of the people who had loved the estate and gardens.

"This was our home, and the town treated it like their property. Teenagers would come in the middle of the night and destroy the flowers. Families would walk into the house as if it was theirs."

"What did your nanny do?" I asked, wanting to know but unable to look at him.

"She was growing pot in a greenhouse," he said, turning to look at the side of my head.

I couldn't meet his eye. "That's not illegal."

He stared at me and didn't have to answer. It's legal now, but it hadn't been then.

"They were threatening to charge my parents and send them to prison to set an example to other rich, entitled people."

"I'm sorry," I whispered, looking down at my empty plate.

"She did this to me with her potions because they turned her in." I didn't understand. "I caught her tending the plants late one night. I was the reason she was arrested and fired."

"Why didn't she go to jail?" I asked, turning to look him in the eyes, my curiosity driving away my shame.

His amber eyes focused on my brown ones.

"Because my parents also paid for her defense and won. She turned around and sued them. When she lost, she cursed me. Her potion turned me into this, and everyone else is gone," he gestured, waving his arms to the house.

"Where are your parents?" I asked.

"Dead. They moved us away after she was arrested, but I wanted to move back after they died. I was here when she lost the lawsuit. I hadn't even wanted to continue it, but my lawyers said we were too far along to give up. I trusted them and now look at me."

I looked at his lips, snarling in his anger.

"Then your father came and plucked the roses he wanted, just like your sisters. I wanted one of them here. The house wouldn't have been so kind to them," he said before pushing back his chair and getting up.

I watched him leave the dining room before I went back to my room and cried. I hadn't done anything wrong, but I had soaked up his anger and sadness as if it had been my own.

* * *

I woke up feeling determined to make life with him bearable. He had spent the last 10 years living as the beast he had been cursed to look like. I was going to help him remember the man he was. His comment about the house allowing my sister to die, if one of them had come here, made me think about what I was allowed. I knew which hallways led to his rooms in the house. They had remained dark since I had arrived a few months ago. I knew a little about the magic, and I knew it wanted to bloom. I was confident it would allow me access so it could reclaim the rest of the house.

I stood at the top of the staircase, where the hallways began, and moved toward his rooms. I could see the magic wake up again as I took each step, the carpet and walls cleaning themselves as I walked. My steps were light and tentative, but the magic responded. I got to the first door which opened, revealing yet another small library. Nicky sat on the floor, next to the fireplace. The fire got brighter as I entered the room, and he looked up at me. His hair was disheveled as though he had just woken up. He was writing in a book, wearing only loose pajama pants. I could see where the beast ended and the man began. His arms were long and sinewed with muscles, his chest and arms covered in the same hair as his mane but not as heavy. I stared and swallowed hard, my mouth suddenly dry.

"What do you want?" he asked when he saw me.

I stretched out both arms towards him, a book I had personally picked for him in my hands. He gracefully got to his feet, stretching as he moved, and slowly walked to me. I could see his tail lazily swaying behind him. He took the book and stood there looking down at me. He was a head taller than me, so I had to look up at him to meet his eyes. I had a sudden desire to touch him, and my now empty hand responded before my brain could stop it. My fingertips grazed the spot on his chest where hair changed to skin, tracing the line across his chest. He shivered when my finger touched him, but he purred. I looked up to see that his eyes were closed.

There was a growing pit in my stomach as my fingers continued down his chest and abs, ending at the waist of his pants. My fingers lingered there as I realized this wasn't fear but desire. I wanted him. I looked up at his face again, and his eyes opened, focusing on my face before he lightly kissed me. It took seconds for our bodies to snap into shared desire, and I wrapped my arms around his neck as his went around my waist. He effortlessly lifted me while I clung to him, my legs wrapped around him. He lowered me to the floor and lifted my sweater off. I felt the light scrape of his nails as he ripped the back of my bra to get it off.

I didn't fight as he removed the rest of my clothes. I felt him move down my body and between my legs, the hair on his face soft against my thighs and his tongue massaging in little circles. How long had it been since anyone had touched him? Never mind how long it had been for me.

As my back arched, my orgasm felt like an explosion, I wanted to make him feel the same thing. I sat up and pushed him back, switching positions as I grabbed the elastic waistband of his pants and pulled. He rose enough to let them slide off and was already hard. I took him in my mouth and heard his breathing get heavy as his orgasm built. He tasted like salt and fire.

I didn't let him have that orgasmic release. I momentarily wondered what the house would provide before I crawled up his body and kissed various spots along his chest, enjoying the feeling of those short, soft hairs on my lips.

"You are so beautiful," he whispered before I pressed my lips to his and pushed him back.

I saw the silver wrappers under the sofa next to us just after he did and watched as he grabbed them. I gave him a moment to get the condom on before lowering myself on him. He fell back on the rug and grabbed my hips as I rode him. I felt one of his hands let go, and his thumb move between my legs, massaging me just before the first, small wave of pleasure moved from my toes and escaped my lips in a moan.

"Callie," he moaned as I rocked faster.

I didn't have time to think about my name on his lips, something I hadn't heard in over a month. Instead, I said something that I was sure he hadn't heard in years. "Nicky!" And my body suddenly exploded in pleasure again.

My knees were unable to do anything but shake when I finally slid next to him by the fire. He rolled over and kissed me. I could taste my body on him and was surprised that it aroused me.

"Tell me to stop, and I will," he whispered as his kisses moved to my neck and down to my breasts.

I said nothing, closing my eyes and focusing on what I wanted him to do to me next. I felt his body on top of me and inside me, thrusting.

"No," I said, opening my eyes.

He stopped moving, but still in a daze of lust. "What?" He asked and pulled out.

"From behind."

I wanted to feel his fingers on my breasts and between my legs. I wanted as many orgasms as he had. He turned me around was quickly inside me again, holding my thigh with one hand while the other massaged my nipple. I felt the sharp intake of breath as I pushed against him, bringing him deeper into me and then felt the hand on my thigh move between my legs. His body fell against mine as we both came, my knees buckled under me. We lay on our sides, and I felt his lips kiss the back of my neck just before I fell asleep in his arms.

* * *

I woke up alone in my bed later that day, still naked, and my clothes carefully folded on my dresser. My mind raced, trying to figure out how I got there. Was it Nicky or the house that had brought me back to my room? I got

63

dressed again, and went to find out, retracing my steps back into Nicky's wing. As I walked, I rehearsed a rant about what behavior I would not allow. When I found him in the same spot I had the last time I walked into the room, I was shut down by the deja vu of the moment. The knowing smile that spread across his face as I walked in quickly fell when he realized I was annoyed.

"Did you bring me back to my room?" I asked.

"Yes," he said in his deep baritone voice.

"Why?"

He swallowed before responding. "I assumed that's where you'd be most comfortable waking up."

The heat rose up my face as I played through different responses. I appreciated his instinct to make me comfortable, but I stumbled over how unexpected all my responses had been that day.

"I don't understand what we are to each other now," I finally said.

He stared at me, not sure how to answer.

"What do you want us to be?" He finally asked.

"I don't know," I said without thinking.

"We could just keep doing this until one of us decided what we want," he said, nonchalantly shrugging.

I didn't respond as he got to his feet and sauntered to me, his tail slowly swinging back and forth. He stopped when there was barely an inch of space between us, and I felt his tail lightly curve around my leg. He raised an eyebrow, pushing me to tell him what to do next.

"I don't want to wake up alone again," I said, looking into his eyes.

"Okay," he said, grabbing my hand as he walked me back to the sofa.

I slid into his lap after he sat down and felt his hand move under my sweater as his lips kissed my neck, his soft hair brushing against my face. I shut my eyes and let him explore.

* * *

"Callie," his whispered in my ear.

We were in my room. We had been here every night for weeks. I knew he wasn't in bed with me. I had felt him get out of it and heard him whisper that he'd be back. I had fallen back to sleep right away.

"Nicky," I whispered with a giggle, his breath tickling behind my ear.

"Do you want breakfast?"

I was beginning to understand how the magic and the house worked. It could move things where it wanted, but it couldn't make things. Nicky ordered food online, the grocery store left it outside the gate, and the magic moved it. Nicky, it turned out, was the one cooking the food. Initially, I was disgusted by the thought of the dirty and unkempt beast as the creature that made such delicious meals. He didn't excuse his behavior. Nicky had almost no regrets. I let go of the feeling quickly, recognizing that it hadn't hurt me.

The magic moved furniture around the house. Nicky's favorite chair suddenly appeared in my room after he had slept here a few nights. I could see light scratches on the leather. Books seemed to move between libraries, and I was sure the bed was now larger to fit both of us comfortably. I wasn't complaining. I was determined to make the most of having to live here. Nicky explored the house with me, explaining what each room had once been and. When the memory made him happy, the room would come alive, repairs quickly happening. If the memory made him sad, the room stayed dark, shades drawn to keep the sun from revealing the disaster it had become.

My favorite room was a sunroom in the back of the house. It was full of plants Nicky tended daily, having inherited his mother's green thumb. As he took care of each plant, talking to them as he worked, I read books. The house had added a chaise lounge to the room where I would relax to read and periodically make love to Nicky. We made love in nearly every room, especially the ones that made Nicky happy, but it was the sunroom that I loved the most.

We lost track of the days, only using the height of the snow against the windows to keep track of time. When the snow finally receded from the windows, I knew that winter was ending. I thought about the grounds before they closed the estate. The cherry trees would bloom first. The world would fill with the bright pink and white bulbs depending on the tree, and the bulb flowers would shoot up from the ground; tulips and daffodils wouldn't last long. In early summer the Maple trees with their helicopter seedpods would fill the world with their sweetness. In July, the summer gardens would go wild, the yellow petals a rosette around the dark brown stem. The roses, if cultivated, would bloom in July and August, the last ones sometimes lingering into Fall.

"I want to bring the roses back," he told me one day after when I walked into the room to find him flipping through a handwritten journal. "The pink ones you loved first."

I walked over to the work table in the room, scattered with empty pots, soil, and fertilizer. He had tinkered with the plants in the room, repotting them as they grew through the winter. This room was warm enough to function as a greenhouse. Over his shoulder, I could see the notes and sketches of flowers someone had created. I knew who the journal had belonged to. I wrapped my arm around his shoulder and kissed the top of his head, inhaling the scent of him.

"The Black-eyed Susans are my favorites. They're like little suns," I said.

He leaned back and looked up at me, his eyes sparkling in a way I would have never recognized months ago. He pulled me into his lap and kissed me as his hands moved up my back. I could feel a low, gentle rumbling of his purr. It vibrated through his body and into mine.

"You smell like them," he said, inhaling deeply and exhaling until there was nothing left in his lungs.

"Like what?" I whispered before kissing him.

"Black-eyed Susans. I used to lay in the field of them, waiting to surprise my mother. She would always be so annoyed that I was crushing them but always laughed when I bounded out at her."

I could see the boy he had been, partly my memory of the dark-haired boy but surprisingly more like a young version of the beast I lived with. I felt his dull claws scratch my back, and I put my head on his shoulder.

"Where did you find this?" I asked, touching the journal.

"It was my mother's notes about the roses. The house revealed it, I assume. It was just here when I came in. It even pulled out some of her supplies. I think I could restore the estate."

"Why?" I asked, feeling overwhelmed with emotions I couldn't explain.

"For you," he whispered, before kissing me.

I pulled away from his lips and looked at him. I felt tears filling my eyes, but I didn't want him to see them. I got off his lap and left the room, hoping to hide until I got my emotions under control again. Nicky followed me, refusing to let me hide.

"What did I do?" he asked, a few steps behind me, careful not to touch me.

He could always read my emotions even better than I could. It had to do with my scent. His body might not be all beast, but his senses were. The curse had transformed him in ways I wouldn't have expected. He was not the bully I remembered from my childhood, not anymore. He knew how I smelled, how I felt under his hands, the color of my skin, the sound of my voice, and how I tasted. He could read every emotional change. I stopped walking and turned back to him, barely able to focus on him through the tears.

"My mother had magic, and it died when she did," I said.

"She did?"

"So did yours but different magic. My mother had words, and your mother had potions. Your nanny was probably hired because she had magic too."

He didn't respond but his tail, which was often curved in a question mark, started quickly and sharply swaying back and forth.

I needed to say what I had been ignoring for months. "I don't have magic, but my mother taught me that magic wants to grow. It can be used to harm, but it would rather make people happy because happy people make babies who spread the magic. The magic in this house is no longer allowing us to be unhappy."

"I don't think this is the magic," he said, enunciating every word.

"It wants you to be happy Nicky. It provided me, didn't it?"

Only his tail moved.

"Is everything we feel something we would naturally feel, or is it the magic?" I asked, holding my hands, palm up, before me as if waiting for something to be placed in them.

"I'm not happy because of the magic," he said, slowly shaking his head. "I'm happy because I love you."

It was like a punch in the gut, but I already knew it. It was what I was feeling, but I didn't know if it was real. I turned around without a word and left him in the hall, alone again. He didn't come to my room that night. I don't know where he slept or if he slept. I certainly didn't sleep. It felt like the magic was punishing me, the beauty of the room fading, his chair removed, and the mattress suddenly lumpy. Maybe the last one was because it had been so long since I hadn't shared the bed with Nicky. When I slept, I dreamed of him changing, shifting back and forth between the beast I knew and the man he would have been without this curse.

I woke up sweating. I got out of the bed and threw open the windows to breath the fresh air, but they quickly snapped shut again and locked. I couldn't reopen it. I went to the door, turning the handle but it didn't budge.

"STOP!" I yelled at nothing. "Let me out!"

The door handle twisted, and the door opened. Nicky stood there, and I collapsed in his arms.

"You're burning up," he said as he lifted me into his arms and walked into my bathroom.

I heard him turn on the water of the bathtub built for two and rip off my nightgown with his claws. They were always just sharp enough to do what he wanted.

"You're sweating so much. It's sticking to you," he said by way of an apology.

I was shivering and felt him lower me into the water. It felt so cold that I started to cry.

"I have you, Callie. It's okay."

"Nicky," was all I could say, tears spilling down my face.

I felt the water move and knew he had gotten in with me. I felt him wrap his arms around me and pull me close to his body. I curled up into the fetal position and fell back to sleep in his arms.

* * *

I woke up to the sound of birds chirping and sunlight streaming into my bedroom. I was back in my bed, wrapped in a towel and Nicky's arms. I could feel his warm breath on the back of my neck and the rumble of his purr against me. I looked around as best I could and realized the sheets were changed, and my comforter was thrown back over the foot of the bed.

"I kept you in the bath until the fever broke," Nicky said behind me.

"Thank you for taking care of me." I rolled over to face him.

He looked exhausted as if he hadn't slept since I had thrown the door open.

"Don't ever say that you don't have magic," he said, meeting my eyes. "You say a word, and I obey you."

"What?"

"You're a very talented spell caster. Sometimes it takes only one word, and I want to give it to you."

I thought back to the commands I had given and his reaction. I thought back to that first night we had been together. I only remembered giving him one direction. When I had said 'no' he had pulled out. How many men would or could do that without complaint?

"I don't want you to obey me!" I said and shot up out of bed.

The room swirled around me, and I sat back down before trying again and getting dressed.

"I don't obey because you command. I do what you ask because you ask so little. I thought about what you said about magic. My mother's magic wasn't potions. It was will. The gardens bloomed because she willed it so. My nanny came to us as part of that will. The curse is my nanny's potion magic."

"The house is part of the curse. It's manipulating me," I said, throwing a sweater over my head.

"No, you don't understand. It's my mother's magic more than mine. You're here because of me, but the house takes care of us because she willed it decades ago. It gives me what I need to be happy because she wanted me to be safe and happy. I demanded that your father send someone here, but I wanted the magic extended to you."

I buttoned my jeans and sat down on my armchair, put my elbows on my knees, and looked at him, naked and in my bed. I turned to the bathroom and saw his wet pajama pants on the floor.

"Do you regret forcing me here against my will?" I asked, as my anger rose.

"No."

I sat back in the chair, not sure how to respond.

"I didn't expect you to be the one to come here," he said, sitting up in the bed. "I expected one of your bitchy sisters."

"My sisters aren't bitches."

"They always were to me," he said shrugging.

"What would have happened if it had been one of them?"

He looked around the room. "None of this. I would only have allowed her to fear me. You weren't the same, and I changed so you could be safe and happy. The moment you told me to sit, in the dining room that night, I knew it was the right decision."

"You just told me I compelled you to sit."

He looked at me and smiled.

"Yes, I feel the pressure to obey when you command me. You've done it, maybe, four times. I obey without resistance because I want to. I know exactly what you want because I love you."

"What if I want to leave?"

"I don't want you to leave," he said as soon as I said the last word.

"I could have left at any time, couldn't I?"

"I don't want that," he said, his voice lowering into a growl.

"I want to leave."

72

I watched his face and felt a shift in the air. I left the room, walked through the house to the kitchen and backroom, where I pulled on a jacket and snow boots. I marched back through the house to the front door, Nicky walking down the stairs in my robe.

"Please don't leave," and I heard the rising panic in his voice. "I love you."

"I want to go home."

"This is your home, Callie. They left you to die," I heard him say behind me.

I didn't respond as I walked out the door and down the path. The gate stood open for me, and I turned back, expecting to see Nicky behind me, but there was only dirty, melting snow.

* * *

I knocked on the door to my family's apartment. The door opened, but I didn't recognize the woman standing there.

"Can I help you?"

I looked past her and saw a room I didn't recognize. The world started to spin, and she pulled me inside and sat me down in a chair next to the door.

"My family lived here," I whispered as the world fell back into place.

"Are you Callista?"

"Yes! Where did they go?"

She looked down at her feet. "They left town. They said you moved away and they were going too. They didn't even leave a forwarding address."

"Did they say they were going to move with me?" I asked, so confused.

She went into the small kitchen and got me a glass of water.

"No," she handed me the glass. "They didn't even go to the same place."

I drank all the water without stopping for a breath.

"Okay, thank you," I got up and left the apartment in a daze.

I heard her voice behind me, but I couldn't make out the words. I wandered through the town, not realizing that I was moving in any specific direction, but within a few hours, I found myself back at the estate's front gate, which slowly opened for me. I shuffled back up the path, and the door opened. Nicky stood there, dressed, and waiting for me.

"They're gone," I said, looking up at him and letting the tears fill my eyes.

"I'm sorry," he said and wrapped his arms around me.

"They didn't even try to tell me," I said and felt the corners of my mouth quiver.

He picked me up and carried me up to my room as I started to cry uncontrollably.

"I didn't know," he said as he walked. "I just assumed they didn't care because they've never tried to see you."

I cried into his shirt, my arms wrapped around his neck. I believed everything he said, he had never tried to manipulate me. I had been happy to forget them as soon as I left the apartment that day. I hadn't really wanted to leave. I never felt as safe and loved after my mother died. That is until I was forced to be here.

"I hate this blue," I said through my tears when we got into our room. "It was my father's favorite color."

"What color do you love?" Nicky asked as he laid me on the bed.

"Purple."

I watched as the colors in the room changed to different shades purple and shifted as if it could see the specific color in my mind. The room was accented with shades of grey and silver, making it seem brighter than it ever had before. Nicky took off my shoes and jacket before kissing my forehead and pulling a light blanket over me. I shut my eyes, and when I opened them again, the sun had set. I could smell something delicious and wandered to the kitchen. I found Nicky over a stove, making soup. I had never actually watched him cook before.

"I found onions and cheese, so I made some soup. I didn't know what else to do."

I sat down at an island I had never noticed before. He ladled soup into bowls, topped with a slice of bread and covered it with cheese before sticking it in the oven. While he waited for the cheese to brown, he poured me a glass of water and put two pills next to the glass.

"To keep the fever away, nothing else," he said, holding his hand up to swear.

I emptied the glass, and he refilled it. The soup was hot and delicious. It was the only thing I had eaten all day. We sat next to each other, quietly eating.

"I like this more than the dining room," I said.

"I don't want you to leave but if you want to, then don't linger."

How long had he waited to say that?

"I love you," he said when I didn't respond. "I've never been this happy. Not in the last 10 years and not

75

in the years before the curse. Everyone has always wanted me to be something specific. I hated that nickname—the prince one."

"The prince without a throne," I said.

"That one. I'm not a prince. I'm moody and hate people who act entitled to what isn't theirs."

"I'm not yours," I said.

I heard him sigh. "No, but I'm yours, and I will be forever."

It was my turn to sigh. "I have nowhere to go, so I might as well stay here."

"There's a whole world, Callie. Just go. Don't say goodbye and don't look back."

"That's what they did," I whispered.

I know he heard me, but he didn't say anything. I got up and helped him clean the dishes. I found a container for the leftover soup and thought about how much better it would probably be for lunch tomorrow. I went back to our room, but he didn't join me. I waited for him to come and make love to me, but I sat there alone for over an hour. I cried a little while I waited.

"He believes he deserves the misery," the magic whispered in my ear for the first time in months.

The hallway between our rooms had never felt so long, but I felt like my mental fever broke with each step. His door was open, and he was lying on his bed, reading the book I had brought him that first night.

"I'm not leaving," I said as I climbed on the bed.

I pushed him back, leaned over him and kissed his lips.

"I'll give you anything you want, Callie. I love you," he said, sitting up.

I straddled him and felt him get hard. I pinned his shoulders against his headboard and made sure to meet his eye. "I love you, too."

I felt a whoosh of power push me back on to my butt as his eyes changed from amber to black, and his hair did the same.

"NO!" I said, trying to command something wild but the magic obeyed, and the air was still, Nicky practically froze as two magics fought for control. I got back to my knees and into his lap. "I don't want the Prince Without A Throne. I want my Nicky. I love you. Like this. Don't change."

I pressed my lips to his and felt the air explode as our combined wills broke the curse our way. When I looked, I saw that he hadn't changed. He was my Nicky, a beast and a man who had no regrets about the mistakes of his past.

Part of Her World
By Rachel Kenley

When Alani woke alone in Maris' bed, she knew exactly where she could find the Sea Witch, even though it was the middle of the night. She stretched her legs, pointing her toes, enjoying the feel of the soft blankets that surrounded her. As a princess of the merfolk realm, Alani was used to luxury and time in landed areas spent without her fin, but there was something particularly lovely about being in Maris' bed. She'd never known she could be so happy with another being.

Of course, that could also be because when the sexy witch shifted from her Oceanide form, a mix of human and octopus, into her fully human body, she frequently kept four arms and two legs which meant more ways for her to touch Alani in multiple places at the same time. The mermaid sighed at the thought of all the ways Maris gave her pleasure. She couldn't tell anyone about her relationship—her family would be shocked on so many levels—but she was so glad to be involved with Maris and liked having a secret from her controlling father. When you were the youngest daughter of six, it was rare to have anything that was your own.

There were two things in Alani's life her family wouldn't understand. Her relationship with Maris and her interest—Maris called it an obsession—with the human realm. Alani didn't think it was really that big a deal, but she did collect things from the bottom of the ocean as well as items she found on beaches. It was such fun to see the things humans used that weren't needed by their counterparts who lived in the Oceans. She found the treasures unique and beautiful. And then there were the people themselves. She couldn't imagine how anyone could be happy with life only on land, but humans seemed to enjoy their limited world.

Alani magicked on a simple dress and went in search of Maris to say goodnight and goodbye. She couldn't stay much longer if she was going to be able to sneak back into the castle unseen. She walked through the rocky halls of the bubbled dwelling—bubbling was how Oceanides created dry areas to live—and eventually arrived at the stairs leading to the laboratory. If Maris thought Alani was obsessed with the human realm, it was nothing compared to how obsessed Maris was with learning and accumulating magic.

She couldn't entirely complain about Maris' focus. If it weren't for their individual interests, they wouldn't have met. Or at least not when they were alone. Alani had seen Maris when she'd come to the castle for events of state because Maris represented her people on the Aquatic council. But her father, King Zale, and the royal security team kept Alani and her sisters away from the Sea Witch and the Cephalonides as well as a few other species. Of course, that made them all the more fascinating to Alani. She'd always wondered about the powerful woman but never imagined they'd meet.

Things between them didn't start well. Alani was looking for detritus from a recent storm when she almost swam straight into the witch. Maris turned around and bellowed, making a sound that rang in Alani's head and startled her so badly she dropped the strange human device she'd found. As it sank into the dark depths of the ocean, Alani pulled herself together and communicated, *That was uncalled for*. When conversing underwater, ocean dwellers were capable of using telepathic communication. Voices were used when air was present.

Maris gave an exaggerated bow, her tentacles swaying around her. *My apologies, dear princess, but I do not like to be bothered as I work.*

The deep, sexy sound of the Sea Witch's voice surprised Alani. Maris swam closer than was polite, staring at Alani. The mermaid had never been so close to a member of Cephalonides. She never realized how beautiful and large the witch was with her dark purple eyes and long white hair which flowed around her. Her body was lush and full, her breasts barely contained by a band of material. Amira ached to reach out and touch her.

What are you doing here, little mermaid, so far away from the protection of your dear father and his army? How did you slip your bonds?

I have my ways, and I'm not so little, Alani said hating how defensive she sounded. She straightened her spine and went on. *It's really not so difficult if you're determined.*

Which clearly you are. How wonderfully surprising. There was a warmth to the other woman's voice which slid over the mermaid's skin and make her tingle. *Don't you like the luxurious world of the castle? Isn't there enough there to keep you busy and interested?*

Maybe for some. Her sisters certainly all seemed to have something they wanted to do. Her mother was a healer and tried to get Alani interested in that but she didn't have the patience. Several enjoyed being in the kingdom's choir, others helped with the children or spent their days in artistic pursuits but Alani found all of those things meaningless or boring. Not that there was much meaning to scavenging for what humans lost, but at least it allowed her to be on her own, finding things no one had ever seen, and exploring places where she wasn't supposed to be. She liked that bit of danger. As long as she was back for the evening meal, no one ever questioned where she was or what she did. They simply assumed she was doing something appropriate for a princess of the realm and didn't ask questions. She didn't liked being easily overlooked, but it had its occasional advantages. Besides, her sisters were willing to chatter about their days and the suitors who had come to meet the oldest two. No one paid much attention to Alani, and she liked it that way.

But Maris did.

Over the course of the next several weeks, Alani kept crossing paths with the Sea Witch. At first she went to some of her favorite places only to discover Maris was there or arrived soon after Alani got there. Then as the weeks went on, Alani found herself looking for the other woman. If she didn't see Maris for a few days she found herself sad and sulky, to the point where her closest sister asked, "Are you in love?"

Alani denied it immediately, but the question made her wonder about her feelings for the Sea Witch.

At every event there were young mermen, and occasionally mermaids because that was acceptable as well, looking to attract the interest of the princesses. Once she'd passed her 21st birthday the year before, Alani was included more and more in that kind of attention. There had been a few times she'd been kissed when she wasn't expecting or wanting it, and there were a few occasions when she was curious enough about the man to make her interest clear and she'd enjoyed the experience well enough.

None of them kissed her like Maris.

She'd been seeing and talking to the Sea Witch for several months, when Maris unexpectedly wrapped a tentacle around Alani and pulled her close. She used a hand to move the hair away from Alani's face, all the while looking into her eyes. There was a moment of shock and hope when Alani knew what Maris was going to do, a moment when she could have pulled away or turned her head, but she didn't want to. She wanted the kiss, and when Maris finally covered her lips, the mermaid quivered in the other woman's arms. Maris' mouth was full, demanding yet sensual at the same time. Alani experienced a moment of surprise when Maris' tongue licked the seam of her lips and she willingly opened her mouth for the other woman. Alani was lost.

It wasn't long after that Maris invited Alani to her home and things moved from kisses and touching to long hours of making love.

Maris' bedchamber was a wonder. The bed was enormous, even bigger than the one her parents shared and covered with the softest of furs and a multitude of pillows. Everything was shades of deepest blue and purple with accents of green. It was lush and bold, just like Maris.

"Don't bother with the dress," Maris said when Alani switched to her legged form. It was automatic to cover herself with material but at Maris' words, she allowed it to disappear and she stood naked in front of the other woman, shivering from excitement and anticipation.

Alani knew she was considered beautiful. She'd been told on many occasions that her blue eyes and long red hair were lovely and that her figure was attractive, certainly the attention she received spoke to that. But she had no idea what a woman like Maris would think of her. Everything about the Sea Witch was big from her voice to her smile to her bosom. Alani feared Maris would find her lacking.

"You look worried, my sweet," Maris said.

"I… I am wondering if now that you see me naked if you still desire me?"

Maris smiled and wrapped Alani in a close embrace. Alani shivered at the cool touch and the strength of the woman she had grown to love. "I desire you a great deal. Never doubt it."

Maris took Alani's hand and walked her to the bed, then scooped her up and put her in the center. "I've waited a long time to have you in my bed, sweet Alani. Since the day we met if you must know, but I admit I never actually thought it would occur."

"I've had a few doubts as well," Alani said. It seemed an important time to be honest. "But I've wanted. I've… fantasized."

"What did you think about?"

"You. Touching me."

"Touching you where?"

"Everywhere," Alani said.

"Sounds perfect." Maris leaned in and kissed Alani deeply as her hands stroked her body paying particular attention to Alani's breasts and only teasing her with wispy touches near her core. Finally, she pulled away from Alani's mouth and moved her head to Alani's breasts, sucking deeply at her nipples, bringing them to hard, almost painful peaks. As she did this, her hand wandered down to the trim curls between Alani's legs, which fell open to welcome her lover's touch.

"I need…." Alani couldn't finish.

"Tell me what you need."

Alani knew if she didn't Maris might stop. "I need to feel you stroke me. Please."

"So lovely to hear you almost begging." Maris slid one then two fingers inside her, and Alani arched her back in an automatic response. "And you're so wet for me."

When Maris moved from Alani's breasts and kissed her way down Alani's body, her breathing became faster in anticipation. Alani had overheard her sisters talk in hushed tones about the delights of oral sex, but nothing prepared her for the rush of sensation she experienced when Maris ran her tongue over Alani's wet opening. Maris' touch brought on a wave of desire so intense it was all Alani could do not to scream.

"By the maker," she managed and gasped at the vibration caused when Maris laughed gently against her skin.

"Indeed. And you're so responsive. It's very sexy."

No one had ever called her that before. It was almost as exciting as what Maris was doing.

Almost.

When Maris slid a finger and then two inside Alani while she continued to lick, the mermaid cried out with the intensity of pleasure that coursed through her. This time the sensation continued to crest, more powerfully than anything she'd ever experienced.

"Don't stop, Maris," she said as the fingers of one hand clawed at the sheets while the other dug deep into Maris' shoulder. As Alani's orgasm neared, Maris pointed her tongue and stroked Alani's clit faster, letting the rhythm of her mouth and fingers bring Alani the pleasure she craved. "Please don't stop."

"Never," Maris said, and Alani screamed as her climax rushed through her. It was like being tumbled by waves, unable to right herself, unsure which direction she was facing.

It was perfect.

When she was able to focus again, Alani found Maris kissing her way up Alani's body. "That was…. You were…"

"It was and thank you," Maris said. "Are you ready for more?"

"There's more?" Alani could hardly imagine what else there could be. Then she thought of it. "Oh yes, let me please you."

"That's for another time," Maris said. "I cannot wait for what I want next."

"Which is?"

Maris turned over and reached for something in

her bedside table. She brought out two polished oblong crystals, rounded at the ends and gradually getting thicker. She handed one to Alani. Before Alani could ask how to use it, Maris had placed the tip at the lips of her opening. The cool stone made Alani gasp and another followed this as Maris slid the crystal deep inside, stretching her. Immediate pleasure followed and Alani understood what Maris wanted.

Giving Maris a soft kiss on the lips, Alani moved her mouth to her lover's jaw, neck, then collar bone and finally licked and sucked at Maris' ample nipples, caressing her breasts at the same time. Hearing Maris' sigh was a thrill. Alani was pleased to discover she loved being able to give pleasure as much as she enjoyed receiving it. In order to reach her goal, Alani needed to stop her kisses and pull away so as to have room. This was quickly done, and as Maris stroked Alani with the crystal she did the same, thrilled to find the other woman was wet and ready as well.

Listening for Maris' responses, Alani moved the crystal inside Maris' core, allowing it to go deeper as Maris moaned deeply. Trying not to focus only on her own pleasure, Alani continued to slide the crystal while finding and stroking Maris' clitoris, loving how the nub became hard and sensitive and how Maris responded.

Soon they were both panting hard, Maris gripping Alani's shoulder so fiercely the mermaid knew she'd have to cover the marks the next day. She didn't care. When she heard and felt Maris surrender to her orgasm, Alani allowed herself to fall over the edge as well. Never had she experienced something to intense with another being.

She couldn't wait for them to do it again. They stayed together for longer than was wise, but Alani couldn't bring herself to leave. Only the fear of getting caught and not being able to return motivated her to go back to the castle.

Over the next few weeks, Alani started to stay home more during the day so she would be rested enough to sneak out of the castle in the evening. This allowed her to spend more time with Maris who was frequently busy during the day not only with collecting things she needed to develop new potions and incantations but having appointments with Oceanides who came to her hoping her magic would help them with their problems or desires.

Alani hated how busy Maris was, hated having to share her with so many people. It was because she was so occupied that Alani met the human prince. A visiting kingdom's royal family was arriving that day for an extended day and Alani didn't know when she'd be able to get away again. She wanted time alone with her lover before being trapped by responsibility.

Maris, unfortunately, was too preoccupied with her work and told Alani to amuse herself elsewhere. It was bad enough to be dismissed that she was frequently overlooked by her family but to have it from Maris was too much. Angry and frustrated, Alani swam away and eventually found herself near a rocky coast. It wasn't a place where she often saw humans, but the waters beneath were littered with treasure from boats that had broken along the cliffs.

Alani was finally letting go of her aggravation and enjoying herself after having found a beautiful heavy necklace she thought would look lovely on

Maris when she sensed pain nearby. Humans couldn't receive telepathic communication but they did send it out unknowingly especially when they were hurt. Coming up from the depths, Alani found a human sinking slowly, blood coming from a gash in his head. There was no detritus from a boat, so she didn't know how he got there but it was clear he was going to die if she didn't help him.

Alani grabbed him around the chest and swam quickly for the surface. Once above the water she stayed in her stronger finned form as long as she could, then dragged him the rest of the way. Leaving him on the sandy shore, she dove back under the water to grab some leaves she saw growing which she knew had medicinal properties. She put the leaves on his wound, then pushed on his chest to push out the water in hopes that he would breath again. She'd learned from her mother that there were times, later in a merperson's life, when the transformation magic failed and water was taken and trapped in the lungs. If they switched to leg form without the magic expelling the water, they died.

When the human started to cough and sputter she moved away, letting him come to on his own. As he lay there unconscious, she hummed to him, a comforting tune her mother used when she was ill. Eventually he started to come to, lifted his head and groaned. "Damn, no more cliff diving" he said putting a hand to his wound. "And what is this?" He pulled the leaf from his cut.

Grabbing his hand, Alani put it back. "You hurt yourself," she said softly. She couldn't believe she was talking to a human. "I put that there to help."

"Thank you," he said. "Ugh, my throat hurts."

"It's the salt water. You took in a great deal, and it's likely burned your throat."

"You pulled me out? Saved me?" She nodded. "Thank you, I don't know what I would have done if you hadn't been there."

"I believe you would have died."

He managed a small laugh. "I believe you're right. I'm glad you came along. Wait, how did you come along? Where did you come from?"

Before she could answer there were distant shouts. "Prince Theodore, can you hear us?" "Where are you?" They were coming closer. It didn't matter to Alani that she was in leg form. She couldn't be found by a group of humans who would ask questions she couldn't answer and possibly take her with them.

"Another time," she whispered to the man called Theodore.

"Wait, don't go. Please," he whispered as she ran toward the rocks in the opposite direction of the voices and disappeared behind them. When she knew she couldn't be seen, she went into the water and finned. Swimming out a safe distance, she broke the surface to look back and used her keen hearing to listen to what the humans were saying. Then men around the prince were worrying about him then trying to help him stand, as he kept asking if they saw the beautiful woman who saved him. They told him his head injury must have caused him to see things.

Once he was gone from the beach, she swam back to her father's kingdom. She thought of seeing Maris briefly to tell her what happened, but she was still mad at the other woman, and she was afraid of her absence being noticed. She arrived in her room only moments before servants bustled in with her dress for the evening. Their guests were interesting, she supposed, and they had a daughter close to her age, but Alani couldn't think about anything other than Prince Theodore and their brief meeting on the beach.

For the next several days were a flurry of events, both social and political, some Alani was required to attend, other times she did things with her sisters and younger members of the family. Mostly, however, Alani did what she could to say in the background, living in her daydreams of seeing Theodore again. Fortunately, her siblings were too busy talking either with or about the visitors and once again, Alani was grateful to go unnoticed.

Maris, on the other hand, noticed immediately. There was full meeting of the Aquatic Council and after it concluded Maris found Alani in one of the secluded grottos.

Hello, my little mermaid, she said surprising Alani. *Are you enjoying all the festivities?*

You know I'm not. How did you find me?

Maris smiled. *I can find you whenever I want you.*

There was something a little ominous in the other woman's words. *Have you done something magical to me? Put something on me or in me so you can track me like one of your lackeys?*

Alani thought she saw a look of hurt on the Sea Witch's face, but it was gone so quickly she couldn't be certain. *Couldn't my love for you be enough of a connection?*

Liking the sound of that, Alani softened and swam over to her lover. She was immediately enveloped in a warm embrace and several limbs. No one could hold her as close as Maris could.

You seemed quite lost in thought just now as well as when I saw you sitting in the balcony during the council. Do you want to share what was on your mind?

She didn't because there was no way she would tell Maris about her interaction with the human. The lie was easy. *I was thinking how frustrating it was to be so close to you but still so far.*

Perhaps the day will come when we can rectify that.

Maris kissed her firmly but as things between them heated up, Alani heard the faint sound of her mother search for her and getting closer. She kissed Maris and darted out of the cavern before they, or her hiding place, could be discovered.

The day after the visitors left, Alani headed back to the rocky shore where she had met Theodore. The area was deserted and although Alani stayed for hours hoping he'd come by, all she got from her trip were a few trinkets she'd found while she dove into the depths to pass the time. For the next several days she visited there first in the hours before sunset, the same time as when they'd originally met, before she swam to be with Maris.

After a week, her patience was rewarded. Theodore appeared on the beach, holding his shoes and looking out onto the horizon. Alani wanted to approach him, but she couldn't think of a way to do it that wouldn't have him asking questions she couldn't answer. If he saw her coming out of the water, he'd know she wasn't human. If she swam to the other side of the rocks and then walked to where he was, he'd ask where she came from. Instead, she came as close as she dared and while still staying out of sight, hummed the tune she'd sung to him when they met.

When he turned around to look, she knew he'd heard her.

"Where are you? I know you must be here. Please, I want to see you again. To thank you. To talk to you."

His words thrilled her, but she couldn't think of how to go to him.

"What do you think of humans," Alani asked Maris one night as they lay in bed together.

"I don't. They are weak, short-lived creatures with whom we must unfortunately share our world. I wouldn't mind if they all disappeared."

"But the things they create, the cities they build. They are fascinating. Surely the people who do those things must be fascinating as well."

"I cannot see how. They are very limited. They can only stay in one form. They can only exist on land. They destroy one another continually. Honestly, I can hardly understand how they've lasted as long as they have."

Alani knew from Maris' tone that she shouldn't bring up the topic any more, but she couldn't help it. The more she spied on Theodore, the more curious she became. Once it had only been their trinkets and treasures, but now she desperately wanted to know more about the man and the world he lived in. What would it be like to walk with him, see his castle, meet his family?

One day when Maris was busy when Alani arrived, she went into the woman's library to see if there were any books on humans. There in the warped bindings she discovered wondrous tales of heroism and adventure that fed her desire.

"What are you reading?"

Alani, startled, slammed the book shut. "Just trying to pass the time until you were available.

Maris glided to where Alani sat and took the book, then looked at the ones scattered on the table around her. "These are stories of humans. Why are you reading these?"

"I was just curious. And bored. You're so busy." She couldn't tell Maris the full truth and knew the best way to distract her. She pressed herself against the other woman and gently kissed her neck. "Are you done for the day?"

As distractions went, it worked well for them both and they spent the next several hours in pleasure. But when Alani left, she tucked one of the novels into a bag and took it with her.

She also continued to make regular trips to Theodore's home, never coming too close but always watching for him, her heart racing when she could see him, and growing to care from him even from afar.

It had been a few months since that first day on the beach when Maris finally said something. "What is going on?"

"What are you talking about?" Alani was helping Maris put things away in her workroom and then they'd go to bed for a few hours.

"You've been distracted for weeks. Even when you're here you're not. It has something to do with that human you've been going to watch."

Alani's instinct was to lie, but she knew that was a foolish move. "So you've been following me?"

"The book you took was marked with magic. I've never tagged you, but I do tag other things. You've obsessed over the trinkets of humans for years. I suppose it was only a matter of time before you obsessed over one of them."

"I am hardly obsessed."

"I've had you followed. I know how often you go to his land."

"How dare you?"

"I dare because I love you."

"If you loved me more you would be so distracted by your work, your magic. Magic can't love you back."

"You are making foolish decisions, Alani. You get too close and risk getting caught because you think of nothing but this male and the world he lives in."

"What do you care," Alani fired back. "You don't have time for me anyway. You're busy, working on something new, selling your wares trying to build wealth that won't buy you anything you don't already have. And it certainly can't buy you time with me which I thought you wanted."

"How dare you. You who grew up with privilege and freedom. You have no idea what it's like to be considered a lesser group, to be looked down on because of something over which you have no control."

"And that's all that's important to you. Your status, how other people view you. What about me, how I view you? How I love you."

"Love? Really? And when are you planning to bring me to the palace to tell your family about our relationship? Will there ever come a time when you introduce me to them? Perhaps it's time to end this, whatever 'this' is."

Alani didn't say anything. Her stomach flipped at the thought of bringing Maris to her home and introducing her as the woman she loved, but it turned equally as much at the thought of losing her. "Maris, please. I don't want to lose you."

"I understand that, princess, but you can't have everything. You want freedom, you want me, and you want to find out more about these humans and the way they live." Maris stared at Alani and something in her gaze chilled the mermaid. "You should have what you want."

Maris stormed off to the direction of her workshop. Alani wasn't sure if she wanted to follow, then decided she needed to know. As she got close, she heard chanting, a language and words she didn't understand but which sounded dark. She stepped in saw Maris' face aglow with a purple light coming from the vial in front of her. When the light dimmed, she capped the bottle, grabbed a shell off a shelf and then came over to Alani, grabbing her by the wrist.

"You're coming with me."

Moments later they shifted out of Maris' dwelling and into the open ocean. Maris swam at full speed, much faster than anything Alani could do on her own. It didn't take long before Alani recognized where they were—the waters near where Theodore lived.

Maris pulled Alani above the waves and dragged her to the beach. They both shifted to legs, and Maris took a step back to face Alani.

"What are we doing? What are you doing?" she asked as Maris began to chant, words that sounded like the ones from the workshop.

When Maris finished what she was doing, she

tossed the vial toward Alani. It broke at her feet and a lilac smoke curled around her body. Something felt as though it was being pulled from her and as she looked at Maris, the witch was holding out the shell she'd brought and Alani thought she saw something wispy going into it. A moment later a chain appeared on the shell and with a wave of her hand Maris was wearing it as a necklace.

Without a word, Maris turned and walked back to the ocean, switching to tentacles the moment she touched the water.

Alani ran after her and tried to shift once the water was knee high.

Nothing happened.

She tried again, but her legs remained. She called after Maris, who was still above the water, and nothing came out.

What have you done to me? she sent. She'd never tried to use telepathy above water and wasn't sure that the other woman could hear her.

Maris stopped and turned. "I've given you what you want. Legs. Permanently. You want to live in the human world, you want to see what it would be like to be with that man, now you can. Enjoy."

Why can't I talk? Maris didn't answer. *What have you done to my voice?*

Maris touched the necklace making the shell glow. "It's safe."

You took my voice? How could she?

"I love you. If I'm going to lose you, I will have something of you to keep with me."

Maris, you can't leave me here. You can't leave me. Two different thoughts, equally terrifying.

96

"Good luck, Alani. I hope you're happy."

She dove under the water and didn't break the surface again. Alani tried to give chase but found her human-only form a weak swimmer. She finally went back to the beach, sitting on the sand, and not knowing what to do. She lay down, curled into a ball and cried, her heart breaking as her fear of her situation overwhelmed her.

She was still there as high tide came in and the waves washed over her. She might have stayed until the water took her back into its embrace when her grief was interrupted by a deep voice

"My lady, are you alright?"

Alani didn't respond, didn't realize the person was talking to her until a warm hand touched her shoulder. She jumped, shifting to a sitting position and pulling away.

"I'm sorry, I didn't mean to scare you. Thank the heavens, it's you?"

She tried to answer, but nothing came out. She put her hand on her throat as tears filled her eyes.

"You poor thing. Was there a shipwreck? I suppose there must have been, and like you told me, you were in the water for too long. The salt water affected your throat. I've been looking for you, hoping you'd return. Come with me to the castle and you'll be taken care of."

When he stood and held out his hand, she took it and let him help her to her feet. He put his jacket on her and the warmth of his body warmed her skin. She breathed in the strange scent of him and tried not to wrinkle her nose at the somewhat acrid smell, so different from the creatures of the sea.

It was not the last disagreeable thing she discovered living among the humans. Each day she was with Theodore she liked the land dwellers less and less. She didn't like their smell or their heavy foods, overcooked and all but tasteless. She didn't like the constant noise from people chattering. And she found that not spending any time swimming made her body feel heavy and almost too solid. She couldn't sleep and longed to float.

Alani hoped she could adjust and learn to like her new life. Theodore was understanding when the doctor informed them that it looked as though she'd never get her voice back. They found other ways to communicate, but Alani often wanted to be alone. It came to a head the night they walked through one of his gardens. He was talking endlessly about the day to day responsibilities of an heir to the throne and pointed out some of the landscape he found beautiful, not knowing that the woman with him had seen much greater beauty. She ached for silence and thought she got her wish when he stopped walking and took her hand. Staring at her he was quiet for a moment, then he leaned forward and kissed her.

Alani was so surprised she opened her lips which he took as an invitation to put his tongue in her mouth. It was awful. Warm and slippery, so different from her beloved Maris. She disliked his taste, his feel. When she put her hands on his shoulders to push him away, he must have thought she was submitting, and he pulled her close, allowing her to feel his arousal through his clothes. His body heated and Alani wanted to run. She missed the cool, soft skin of her lover. The warmth of these humans was suffocating. She couldn't stand being near it another moment.

Finally managing to step away from him, she put a hand to her lips resisting the urge to wipe his touch away. Again, he misread her actions.

"I'm sorry. Perhaps I shouldn't have been so bold, but I wanted you to know how drawn I am to you, how I've grown to desire you in addition to enjoying your company. I look forward to the time I spend with you every day. I hope you feel the same."

For the first time Alani was glad she didn't have a voice because she had no idea how to respond, and if she told him the truth, who knows how he would react. He could send her away, and there was no way she could survive alone in the human world. She was trapped. She gave him a slight smile and took his hand, allowing him to lead her back to the castle where he kissed her again before they said good night.

For the next several days Alani tried to enjoy her time with Theodore, tried to like his kisses and the way he touched her, but it was no use. Night after night she'd walk along the beach, longing to dive in and swim away, longing for her love, sending message upon message out into the vast ocean hoping someone would hear, that someone would take her away.

But there was no answer. She was alone. And she was exhausted. Finally she decided she'd rather be foam on the waves than spend one more night among the humans.

The next day at sundown, Alani stood on the edge of the cliff prepared to jump as Theodore had, prepared to die as he would have if she hadn't saved him. Foolish little mermaid.

As she was about to step out there was a deep cry from the water below. "No, my daughter, don't."

Alani looked down and saw her father and family above the waves. Tears filled her eyes. This only proved her decision was right. She could never be with them again. Better to end it all. She stepped off the land and let the air embrace her.

"Save her," she heard him yell.

Alani looked and to her surprise and horror she saw Maris beside her father. Before she could react or send out a last goodbye, the Sea Witch raised her hands and magic flowed between them. With a flick of her wrists, Maris released the magic and moments later it encompassed Alani in light and power. It passed through her, and Alani was grateful her end would be swift.

Except it wasn't.

As she hit the water her body immediately transformed back into her original form. The sensation of having a fin again was one of the most wonderful things she'd ever experienced. She swam quickly to the surface to tell her father she was well and when she did she was relieved to hear her voice again. As he wrapped her in a loving hug, she looked over her shoulder to Maris, who nodded.

"I cannot believe you went to the humans," Zale said when he finally released her. "I never thought your interest would have you make such a foolish decision. We could have lost you forever. I have forgiven Lady Maris for giving you the magic which put you among those terrible beings." It wasn't quite the truth, but Alani didn't care. She was home.

"And," Maris said. "Our bargain, King Zale."

Alani's father sighed. "I'm sorry to tell you this, daughter, but to get you back, Lady Maris and I have made a bargain. She agreed to use her magic to return your form, and I agreed release you into her custody for the next decade, after which time you may return to us."

Alani could have squealed with pleasure, but since her father had no idea he'd granted her fondest wish, she bowed her head and nodded. "I understand, father. My choice must have consequences."

"You are to come back to the castle with us tonight, pack, and your mother will deliver you to the Sea Witch's realm in the morning."

It was the longest night of Alani's life. She played her part, reacting appropriately weepy as her family came to bring her trinkets and offer sympathy but as soon as she'd been left with Maris she jumped into the other woman's arms and kissed her deeply.

"Never let me go again. Never send me from your side. Let me be with you always."

"Now that is something I am happy to do for you. For us both."

Rumpled
By Trevann Rogers

Rhiannon cupped her mug of honeybush tea and leaned back against the London plane tree. Autumn nights had always been her favorite. The air was cool, and on the clearest evenings, she could see stars.

She remembered tales of a time before Unakite City. Before the too hot pavement and too cold steel. Her kin had owned all the land from the water to the tallest hill. As time passed and humans selfishly populated the planet, their acreage became smaller and smaller. When the last of their land was taken and a building raised, her family had nowhere to live except inside it, hiding from those who had murderously staked a claim on their property. Centuries later, she lived alone in the only home she had known.

She took a sip of her warm treat. At once a part of the earth and the heavens, in nature, she felt at peace in a way she did not when she was surrounded by brick and mortar. Sadly, the lot behind the behemoth of a building was the only nature she dared visit.

The sun peeked over the horizon. Birds and cicadas loudly welcomed the dawn, stressing the need to return to her lair beneath the latest of many structures that humans had built on her land. She patted the grass and said goodbye to the daylight, and then hurried inside.

* * *

Shelly turned off the burner just as the stew threatened to bubble over the sides of the orange enameled pot. She scooped up a spoonful of the thick, steaming liquid and touched it to her lips. Too hot.

She blew across the spoon several times and took a tentative sip. "Damn, that's good." Dancing across the kitchen, she sang to her father. "Dad, it's delicious! Come and eat! It's your favorite, what a treat!"

Bob slid into the room in holey white socks and grabbed her into a spin, twirling her to the made-up song. He was as silly as she was. At a robust 6'2", he was a few inches taller than her, and she could dance with him without feeling like a freak. Not that she did much dancing with anyone else these days.

She laughed and wriggled out of his arms. "Dinner's ready, and you need to leave soon."

"Fine, Partypoop." He inhaled deeply, his full, gray mustache accentuating his grin. "Chicken and dumplings. Smells just like when your mom used to make it."

She kissed his cheek. "Let's hope it tastes like hers, too." She ladled two bowls of the rich stew and handed one to him. "Your drink's by your chair."

He dropped into the recliner and flicked on the remote before taking a mouthful. She wished he wouldn't watch TV while they ate dinner but shows about exotic places drew him in like a thirsty man to water, and it was time for his favorite. He'd worked hard for so many years, but between putting her through school and the massive medical bills they'd racked up because of her mom's illness, there was never time, opportunity, or money to do something as decadent as taking a vacation.

She sat on the sofa and pulled a throw around her shoulders. "I wish you didn't need to work tonight. Don't you want even one day off?"

He shook his head while he swallowed. "Why? I like what I do, and most of the people there are my friends. You know we can use the extra cash."

Shelly winced as her hands started to ache. She set down her bowl and spoon and bent each finger at the knuckle until the tension released with a satisfying crack.

She shouldn't have quit her job until she had another one lined up, but she'd had all she could take. Designing creative marketing plans for companies that cheated customers or made a product so inferior it couldn't withstand the photoshoot was like trying to make a pile of crap smell like a daffodil. She'd walked away from the whole enterprise two months ago when the Young Again, Tools for Assisted Living Corporation joked about an older woman who'd sued them for an injury she sustained using their shoddy and expensive portable commode.

"I'm doing the best I can, Dad. I submitted a few applications."

His eyes narrowed, and he put his bowl on the end table. "You know I didn't mean it like that. I was talking about me. You should hold out for a job that makes you happy."

"I want to work for a company that cares about making a difference, not just about money."

He took her hand in his. "Take your time, sweetheart. We're doing okay. The best job will find you. In the meantime, could you try to have some fun? You never seem to enjoy yourself."

"What are you talking about? I have plenty of fun."

"When was the last time you saw a movie? Went to a bookstore? Had a dinner date?" He held up his hand when she started to protest. "With someone besides me. Find some excitement, Shell. What was your mom's favorite Prince quote? From when he won that award. *"Life is death without adventure.""*

Shelly took a deep breath and puffed out her cheeks before slowly letting the air out. He was right. Since quitting her job, she had no desire to do anything but cook, hang out with him, and try to figure out what to do with her life. After 26 years as his daughter, however, she knew better than to argue with him about this.

"I promise to increase my adventure quotient." Somehow.

* * *

She'd been right. Her dad was exhausted. He'd fallen asleep after lunch, something she'd never seen him do. Then, late for work, he jumped up, jammed on his boots, and ran out of the house. He sped off, forgetting the lunch she'd packed for him.

She turned into the company parking garage and began the climb to higher floors. Everyone at Temptation Records worked long hours, not just her father. At 6:00 people should be going home for the day, but there were no empty spaces on the lower

105

levels. Finally parked, she made her way to the lobby and secured a visitor pass before heading to her father's office.

The record company's vibe was moneyed and modern, but she thought it harsh and impersonal—glossy walls lined with elaborately framed music awards, white marble floors, and gleaming chrome fixtures. Pulling her sweater tightly around her, she lowered her head and hurried down the corridor.

"Shell!"

Startled, she stumbled and pitched to the right.

"Whoa," her father chuckled as he caught her before she crashed into a potted fern. "You okay? What are you doing here?"

Still, in his arms, she frowned and handed him his lunchbox. "You forgot—oh."

Heat rose to her cheeks. She stood and brushed back her hair with her fingers, wanting to kick herself for not taking the time to find something better to wear than her sweatpants.

The man standing by her father was a head shorter than her, his expensive suit tailored for his stocky yet athletic build. He probably played football in college. He smirked and extended his hand.

"Larry. Larry Rudenstine. And you are... ?"

"Shelly." She expected a firm handshake like her father's, but his clammy fingers barely grasped hers and then slid away.

"Oh, jeeze, I'm sorry. Shelly, this is Mr. Rudenstine, President of A & R. Artists and Repertoire. Mr. Rudenstine, this is my daughter, Shelly. She's as gifted as she is gorgeous."

"Is that right?" His leer traveled from her eyes to

her breasts, to her feet, and back to her breasts. "I'm always interested in new talent. Do you sing?"

Her father beamed. "Does she sing? Like a songbird. You should hear her."

"I'm sorry, Mr. Rudenstine. My father…"

"Call me Larry. I insist."

Shelly nodded and swallowed hard. All she wanted was to give her dad his food, go home, and drown her humiliation in a pint of ice cream. Preferably chocolate.

"Please forgive him. He tends to exaggerate."

"You're modest. You'd make a beautiful album cover." Larry walked a slow circle around her. "Tall. Blond and blue-eyed. Nice body. Not bad looking." He licked his lips. "I'd love to hear you sing."

She leaned away from him, bile rising in her throat—what a creepazoid. "No, thank you. I'm good."

"C'mon, Shell. Just a little something. What was that song you were humming this morning?" Her father rocked back and forth on his heels, grinning.

What the hell did he think he was doing? They'd sung off-key together since she was a kid. She stuck a toothy smile on her face, one she used to charm her vilest clients. "All of my singing happens in the kitchen or the shower." She winced, wishing she could take back the shower image. "Or the car."

"Fascinating."

"What's that song I like? By that girl, Taylor something?"

"Dad, stop. Please." She tried to sound firm, but the whine in her voice betrayed her.

"How sweet. You're shy." Larry stroked his beard with his thumb and forefinger. "Come back tonight. We dwindle to a skeleton crew around 10, so no one will watch you or listen in. You have my word. Just lay down a track for me. I'll let you use one of the small studios. "

Bob's mouth hung open. He stared at his boss. Shelly was just as shocked.

"Excuse me? No." Shelly shook her head at her dad. "Uh, uh. No way."

"Give me a chance to persuade you. I'm not used to hearing no. "

That was not a surprise. "Sorry. Music is not my thing."

"Tell me what is."

"She's a marketing executive, but she's between jobs at the moment."

"Dad!"

"Tell you what. I'm feeling generous." Larry put a hand on her shoulder and squeezed gently. "Give me one track. I'll suggest your dad for a raise and you for an interview with the VP of Marketing."

Shelly covered her eyes with her palms. She'd have to pick up two pints. Double chocolate brownie. "This cannot be happening," she whispered to herself.

"Shell, a raise. And a job. Besides," her dad nudged her with his shoulder and whispered, "Where's your sense of adventure?"

Great. He pulled the Mom card. How was she supposed to say no?

* * *

Rhiannon lay on her cot with Albert on her belly, one hand on him and the other holding a copy of a book she'd found in the restroom. Both of their stomachs growled. "Soon, kitty. Let me finish this chapter." He purred as she stroked his white fur.

She loved to read. The world had changed so much, and books had been an easy way to keep up with human advances and upheavals. She particularly enjoyed fairy tales about her kin, the Fae and other magical beings. They were usually quite funny. Humankind had an inflated notion of its superiority and seemed obsessed with happy endings.

Books also kept the loneliness at bay. Through them, she would reminisce about her childhood and life in a simpler time. Today's world was too complicated. Outside these walls, she'd faced unknown dangers without respite. Without friends.

Enough lamenting. Time to eat. She sat up and stretched, and then donned her favorite jacket, pulling the hood up and around her face. It enabled her to blend in, as well as spare the humans the sight of her. Her people were not known for their aesthetic appeal.

She climbed the stairs to the eighth floor. It was a long way from her enclave off the boiler room, but despite the years since the old building had been updated to include the elevator, a gadget that flew people to different levels, she still didn't trust it. Nature's way was best, always. If she wanted to eat, she'd take a walk.

With a wave of her hand, the steel door opened, and she peered out of the vestibule. The day was short, and few humans remained. None of them lingered in the food place called Cafe after the sun went down.

She headed first to the electric icebox, her favorite modern convenience. This one housed all manner of cheese, white cheese, yellow cheese, a cheese with surprisingly delicious mold. Today she found stone fruit and with the cheese, she had a veritable feast. Next, she went to the vast cupboard. Bags of tea leaves, bread, a jug of water, a jar of cherry jam. Fish in a can for Albert.

Stopping at one of the supply closets, she grabbed a light bulb and a few other essentials and happily sprinted down the steps with her bounty.

Albert mewled with irritation, winding in and out around her legs as she dished out his tuna.

"You would receive your food faster if you did not make it so difficult for me to move."

After setting his bowl on the floor, she scooped cherry jam onto a slice of bread and slid down the wall next to him. In the quiet of their meal, she listened to the faint echoes from the music rooms. The only positive side effect from humans inhabiting her home was the stream of melodious sounds they produced, all pleasant to her ears. Many an evening she'd sat on the stairs adjacent to the room where instruments were played, and humans sang. Music, in all of its varieties, had been a part of the world since there were creatures in it. It connected her to human beings—it seemed the one thing they had in common.

His belly full, Albert fell promptly asleep on her pillow as usual. He would be no fun at all for the next few hours. Still hungry and more than a little restless, she quietly grabbed some more bread, a bit of white cheese, and a peach, and headed toward the music.

* * *

Facedown on the small leather couch, Shelly groaned, opened one eye to check the time, and groaned again. She'd been in the studio for three hours so far, and all she'd managed to record was a nasal, discordant rendition of the Mr. Rogers' theme song. Damn that carton of double fudge brownie deliciousness. Dairy always clogged her nose.

Against her every rational thought and gut instinct, she'd agreed to Larry's challenge. If her father got the raise promised, and if she had a line on an interview, she would remember tonight as the moment she dared to step into a successful adventure. If she didn't pull it off, it was going to be another embarrassing mistake in a bevy of mistakes.

She pushed up and dragged herself to the soundboard in the adjoining room. No way would she give up now. She pressed the button the recording engineer had marked "THIS ONE" and started to sing.

"What is wrong with you?"

Her heartbeat pounding in her ears, Shelly's mouth shut mid-note. She scrambled out of the chair and kicked it away, her fists up and ready.

"I asked you a question." The trembling voice rattled the recording booth's glass partition.

Shelly cried out, grabbing her head in her hands. "Stop! Please! I'll answer."

When the throbbing pain subsided, she fell to her knees, gasping. "Nothing is wrong. I'm recording a song."

Easily eight inches shorter than Shelly, the creature wore a wrinkled burgundy hoodie which obscured its face, with spikes of black hair jutting out. Add timeworn black skinny jeans and high-top sneakers, and the look was fairly typical. Except for the layer of... was that cat fur?

"Do not look at me." Its volume lower and tone softened, it waved a hand and dimmed the lights before picking up the overturned chair. "I have been listening to you. You do not sound like a singer." It sat at the soundboard.

Shelly stood slowly, keeping an eye on the rumpled little creature. "I'm not, but I'm trying my best." She blurted out the whole story and shrugged. "I don't have a choice. I've made a promise to record a song, but I'm terrible."

"I can help." In a flash it was standing at Shelly's side, lifting a strand of her hair. "Your locks are much like straw. I can spin them into gold. It would be quite easy."

Shelly started to laugh but choked it down and coughed instead. This rumpled thing with the stilted speech pattern was insane. Better not make it angry. "That's quite a special talent. Thanks for the offer, but I like my hair. Wouldn't know what to do with a scalp full of gold anyway. What I need is a song, reasonably sung, by the time my dad and his boss get here in... " She rechecked the clock and frowned. "In four hours."

"Fine. I will sing for you."

The memory of the burning pain in her head almost knocked her to her knees again. "No," she said more forcefully than she intended. "I mean, I appreciate the kindness, but I would hate to put you out or anything."

"Not a gift, a favor. After which you will owe me one."

"Again, thank you, but..."

"It is done. What shall I sing?"

Maybe if she humored it, it would go away quickly without hurting her. She simply needed enough time for one more go at it herself.

"Okay. Thanks. You choose the song." She pulled another chair beside the recording equipment. "Whenever you're ready."

The little creature sat back in the chair, sighed, and started to sing.

I wander the earth and the underworld,
Alone, and barely alive.
Searching for a reason to carry on.

It filled the room with its powerful voice, perfect notes beautifully sung.

A chill moved through Shelly. She didn't so much hear the song as felt it resonate inside her. As the melody progressed from despair to hopeful, so did she. By the time the creature finished, only joy had remained.

"Well, damn," Shelly sniffed and wiped her eyes with the tip of her finger. "Your voice is breathtaking. I love all kinds of music, and I've never heard anything like that before."

She extended her hand in a friendly gesture, but the creature withdrew. "I'm so sorry. I'm a toucher. I won't do it again." Shelly sat on her hands to make sure of it. "I only wanted to show you how moved I am by your voice. Can I ask you something?" Taking the silence as a good sign, she continued. "What are you? An alien?"

The creature tugged at its cuffs. It looked

nervous. "Of course not. I am what you would call a troll."

A troll? She'd read stories with trolls in them, but she'd never suspected they were real. "Do other magical beings exist? Like dragons?"

"I have never met a dragon. Fairies, goblins, and huldu are my kin."

"I had no idea." She was pretty sure no one else did either. "I'm Shelly. Shelly Goodman. What's your name?"

"If you give someone your name, it can be used to wield power over you. I now know yours. You will not know mine."

"Never heard that before, but I have to call you something. What if I need to get your attention?"

"I do not care what you call me."

"Fine. I'll call you Rumple," she grinned. "It suits you. Would you mind singing that song again? This time I'll remember to press the record button."

* * *

Shelly paced the small room, rubbing her hands. Her father told a whopper of a story about her supposed talent, and she learned that supernatural creatures were real. She hadn't believed anything more could happen to make this week any weirder. She'd been wrong.

As soon as they'd arrived, she'd played the track for her dad and Larry. Her dad cried. Boy, did that sting. If he thought about it, he'd know it wasn't her voice. Not that she regretted her decision. She'd do whatever she needed to do. Besides, if she admitted the truth—that a troll showed up with a soul-soothing voice and offered to help her out—who would believe her anyway?

Larry, on the other hand, had the wide-eyed, frenzied look of a child who'd realized there's more candy in the trick or treat bag than he could eat. Shelly almost heard the *cha-ching* of the cash register in his head.

He called in two junior members of the legal team and presented a contract to her that would tie her to the company for two albums with a small initial advance and a minimal percentage of sales. She told him she'd think about it. She'd need a lawyer to look at the agreement.

His entire demeanor changed. No longer giddy and smiling, he tossed back a few antacids and sent his attorneys away. He wanted to hear her voice, live, and in person. She again refused to sing on the spot. Demanding assurance she didn't cheat or dupe him, he insisted on locking her in the studio overnight with only the recording equipment, snacks, and her cell phone, in case of an emergency.

With her father's encouragement, she consented, but her thinking had been so flawed that her brain must have momentarily stopped working. With the doors secured, even if the rumpled creature came back—and that was a long shot of the highest magnitude—the troll wouldn't be able to enter the studio to help her.

She grabbed her right fist with her other hand and squeezed until she felt the familiar *pop*. It was 5:00 a.m. No more time to pace or worry. She had to get down to business and sing. Emerging empty-handed would be worse than playing them her imperfect-but-totally-acceptable-in-the-shower stylings. She hummed the introduction to Mr. Rogers theme song and hit the record button.

"That is not a good song. It sounds quite juvenile."

Shelly flinched, choking mid-lyric, and spun the chair around. The troll had terrible timing, and apparently an unending supply of rumpled, haired-over burgundy hoodies.

"It's supposed to. It's a song for children. How did you get in here? The door's locked."

The troll tilted its cloaked head. "This is my home. No room is unavailable to me."

"You live here?"

Rumple nodded. "Yes. My family had lived here since before this structure was erected."

Shelly stretched the fingers in her right hand before taking the fist in her left and squeezing. *Pop. Pop. Pop.* "They live here?"

"Not anymore." The troll took a step back. "What are you doing? That sound is nauseating. Did you break your bones?"

"I cracked my knuckles. No, not actually cracked. More like released some of the gasses in the spaces between my joints."

Shelly stayed as still as she could while Rumple took her hand and slowly turned it over as if examining it. The creature's hands were small. Soft. Feminine.

The troll was a woman.

For the first time, Shelly studied her face. Pale, nearly translucent skin. Big hazel eyes that sparkled even in the dim studio light, and her lips... Holy cow.

"Why must you expel this gas?" Rumple stroked her fingers. Her touch was delicate but not tentative.

Wait. What was happening? It had been forever since someone had flirted with her, let alone touched her so sensuously, but Shelly remembered it feeling like this, warm and tingly.

She glanced away and took a deep breath. "Because my hands get stiff sometimes. It helps them loosen up. I also do it when I'm nervous."

"Do I make you nervous?"

Shelly nodded. "From the minute I first met you."

The small creature held Shelly's hand between both of hers. Warmth seeped into her fingers, and spread up her arm, across her chest, and down the other arm.

Rumple put her hands back in the pockets of her hoodie. "Do you want me to sing for you again? You are much better today, but you still do not sound like a singer."

"Yes, please." Shelly studied her fingers. No more ache. "Larry—I told you about him, right? He wants another song before he'll agree to my dad's raise. Instead of an interview, he offered me a recording contract."

"You would owe me two favors. More, if I keep singing for you."

"What do you want?"

"You will give me a share of your riches. Forty percent from now through eternity. And I will have your firstborn child."

"My what?"

"You will have many. The first one will be mine."

She gasped. "Why do you want my child? Are you going to... to eat it? Or... "

"That is none of your concern. Yes, or no?"

Trade her child for money? This was the 21st Century, not the 16th. The idea was not only disgusting but illegal.

She had to think quickly. No way could she keep this shady agreement. Maybe it wouldn't hurt to say yes for now. She'd back out once the recording contract was signed, citing legal technicalities and then she'd offer Rumple another two or three percent of royalties.

"Alright, fine. Forty percent of my royalties and my firstborn. But we have to hurry. I'm out of time."

* * *

Rhiannon's heart raced. People had started to enter the building, and she needed to get home before the humans noticed her. Several people had gathered in front of the stairwell closest to the music room, talking about a concert from the previous night. She pulled her hoodie down over her eyes and slipped by them nonchalantly.

The next stairwell was open. She bounded down the steps two at a time into the bowels of the building, sprinted around the ducts and pipes, and finally landed at her hidden quarters.

She closed the door carefully and leaned against it, trying to catch her breath. She had never been above ground at this hour of the morning. The human, Shelly, had done something to her to make her act so recklessly. Judging from the warmth of her skin and the trembling she could not control, Shelly had poisoned her. There was no other explanation for touching the human, let alone healing her hands.

And what had possessed her to tell her the truth about the Fae? She'd given this human knowledge their hostile race had all but forgotten.

Her stomach roiled. It was she who had been aggressive. Had she really claimed the human's firstborn child? Not since her ancestors' time had that been done—and it had been frowned upon even then. Only evil trolls engaged in such horrors. Shelly likely thought her a monster, believing she wanted to harm the child in some way. Or to eat it.

She needed to apologize and tell her the pathetic truth. She was merely lonely. In fact, she didn't mind singing for the human. She'd rather enjoyed her company and would assist her without the favors owed.

The money would be useful. She would be able to acquire a place to live, close to nature and away from humans where she could again see the sun. She would invite Shelly to visit her, and they would sing many songs together.

Her legs buckled as the memory of Shelly's soft skin overwhelmed her. She'd awakened feelings long forgotten. She liked holding her hand. She would hold it again if permitted.

"Come here, kitty." She settled into the rocking chair and pulled a blanket over her lap. Alfred jumped onto it and snuggled down.

Much too warm to engage the heat, she flicked on the electric hearth. The soft light of the make-believe flame comforted her. She'd pet her boy for a while, then make a cup of tea and eat a bit more bread and cherry jam. There was no more that could be done today. Tomorrow looked promising.

* * *

Larry upended the bottle of antacid and swallowed half of the chalky tablets without chewing. Over the past three hours, they'd gone over a standard new artist contract and reviewed each clause. The last item was arguably the most important: The cash.

"No, Shelly. I cannot, and I will not give you, a brand-new singer, a majority cut of the royalties. The best I can do is a 40% share."

"Then I want $100,000 in advance," she demanded. She assumed he'd counter offer half that. "And the raise for my father when I sign the contract. You promised him, so that's not negotiable."

"That is an obscene amount of money for a new artist."

She shrugged. "I don't know anything about that."

He pulled the handkerchief from his jacket pocket and dabbed his forehead. "You'll have to earn out your advance, which will take you years and multiple albums." He stood and extended his hand. "However, I can agree to it with an increase in your obligation from two to five albums. Copies of the contract will be sent to you and your attorney via courier by the end of the day. It's an unprecedented deal. We'll have a celebration tomorrow night. You can sign the contract at that time and meet your team."

Holy cow. After giving Rumple her cut, she'd net $60,000. "Yes, I'll be here. Thank you for the opportunity."

She left his office, pumping her fist in the universal victory sign, but close to her side so no one could see it.

"Dad! The lawyer's on the phone! Come on, he doesn't have a lot of time."

Bob jogged into the living room and sat next to Shelly on the couch. She put her cell on speaker and laid it on the coffee table. "We're both here, Mr. Stauton. What do you think?"

Much like Larry had predicted, the attorney said sign it quickly because a good deal like that wouldn't be offered twice. As soon as she clicked off the phone, Bob jumped out of his seat.

"You're going to be rich, Shell! Woohoo!" He swept her into his arms. "I have to tell you, I was teasing when I told Larry you were a singer. I was surprised you said yes." He kissed her forehead with a loud smack. "I never realized you had pipes like that. I mean, you and me, we're always singing something. But your voice came to life in that studio."

After sending her dad off to the bar where he would probably brag to his friends, Shelly curled up on the sofa. His words echoed in her head. He was right. Marketing was her passion, not music. He was also wrong. The otherworldly vocals belonged to Rumple, not her.

At first, she'd been afraid the troll would kill her. But Rumple hadn't hurt her, and it was she who'd taken a defensive stance first. Maybe the troll had been frightened, too.

And then, they touched. A bit of something magical or a soft, seductive caress that healed her inflamed fingers? It didn't matter. It was a caring

121

gesture. Not the behavior of someone who would want to eat a child.

Shelly sat up and held her head in her hands. She'd almost forgotten. She'd stupidly, greedily agreed to give up her firstborn child in exchange for the song. Not that she would go through with it. She had planned to secure the contract then tell Rumple the deal was off. Maybe she didn't understand she couldn't sell a person in 2020. In any case, Rumple didn't deserve to be manipulated. It was time to come clean and apologize.

Although it was nearly midnight and few people were in the building, no one seemed concerned that Shelly was roaming the halls unaccompanied. If you acted confidently, people assumed you belonged and that you knew what you were doing.

She took the elevator to the basement. The dark, humid space was daunting and spanned the width and length of the whole building. Taking a cue from a few procedural television dramas, she mentally divided the floor into a grid and methodically began searching each square. In the middle of the third quadrant, her flashlight flickered and dimmed.

"Goddamn motherfucking..." Without a light, she might not find her way back to the stairwell, let alone see Rumple. Keeping close to the wall, she inched her way around the basement. It would take her all night to cover the whole floor. She squinted against the darkness, looking for an exit sign.

A glow emanated from a seam in the wall. She wouldn't have seen it if her flashlight had been working. As she approached the light, she heard a soft voice singing.

I will always win this game,
They don't ever guess my name.
Albert knows it can't be done,
For I am called the Rhian-non.

Rhiannon. How beautiful. She whispered into the fissure. "Hey, it's Shelly. Are you in there, Rumple?"

The wall dissolved and revealed an open door. Shelly looked into the small space: A cot took up one corner, layered with pillows and colorful blankets. Several bookcases, a rocking chair, and a small electric fireplace filled the center room. The far corner contained what seemed to be a pantry.

Rumple's tiny home suited her. It was warm and cozy and uncomplicated. Nothing, however, was as stunning as Rumple. Rhiannon.

Her hair was longer than Shelly expected. Black, wrinkled skinny jeans as always but instead of her usual hairy hoodie, she wore a camisole. It was also burgundy. At least some things were consistent. It clung to her compact yet curvy frame.

Shelly shook her head to clear up her wandering thoughts. "Your home is lovely. I hope you don't mind that I came to find you."

Rhiannon gestured for her to come in. "No, I looked for you earlier tonight. I thought you might be in the studio. I am happy to see you."

Shelly's heart fluttered. "Me too, you."

"Please have a seat. I have something I would like to say."

Shelly took the rocking chair. Rhiannon sat on the floor by her feet; a fat white cat sauntered into her lap.

"I am not sure why I said it, but I will not ask you

for your child in exchange for my help. I grow weary of being alone. I do wish for children someday, but not like this. It is enough for you to pay me for my services."

"We've been thinking about the same thing. When I agreed, I knew I wasn't going to give you my child. I could never do it. Even if I wanted to, the law wouldn't let me."

Shelly made a fist, preparing to crack her knuckles, but Rhiannon took her hand, and the tension slipped away

"I was going to pretend otherwise until I signed the contract, and then break my deal with you. But I couldn't. You've been kind to me, and I like you. Even though on the day we met, you gave me the worst headache of my life."

"I did not mean... I would never have... "

Shelly leaned forward and kissed the smaller woman. "That was way out of line. I'm sorry." She started to get up and leave, but Rhiannon still held her hand.

"Wait." She shooed the cat from her lap and knelt, her hands on Shelly's knees. "Would you consider doing that again? The kiss?"

"Oh, yes."

* * *

The chamber adjacent to the A&R office overflowed with people. Shelly didn't recognize most of them, but her dad was there, along with the legal team and a photographer. Finger foods of every type sat on sterling trays and in porcelain bowls. She chuckled at the variety of cheese boards. Rhiannon would be impressed.

Funny what you learned about someone when you stayed up all night talking.

"Shelly," Larry waved at her from across the room. When she joined him, he put a meaty arm around her and grinned. "Ladies and gentlemen, may I have your attention? Allow me to introduce our guest of honor and the newest artist under the Temptation label, Shelly Goodman."

The room erupted into cheers and applause as Larry presented her with flowers and a gold pen. He might be a sleaze, but as a leader, he knew what he was doing. Throwing a party to bring a new person into his stable of talent would make anyone feel welcome. It made her feel like a fraud.

Her dad hugged her and whispered into her ear, "What's wrong, sweetheart? You look like you're going to cry. I know music wasn't what you'd planned, but here it is. Try to enjoy the moment. It's all for you."

It wasn't her moment. It belonged to Rhiannon. "Dad, I think I have to choose a different adventure. Maybe a life-changing one."

He nodded and hugged her tighter. "Is it's going to be fun?"

"I think so."

"A little scary, a little risky?"

"Probably." Tears ran down her cheeks as she laughed. He was the best dad, ever. "If it works, you might be able to take that tropical vacation you've wanted."

"Fortune favors the bold, baby. Do it."

"I love you, Dad." She glanced around the room and found Larry huddled in a corner with the photographer. Perfect. "Cover for me."

She bolted out of the party and down the nearest stairs.

* * *

Rhiannon yawned as she opened her door, her hair tousled. "Hi, Shelly. Did you sign the contract?"

"Where's the camisole you wore last night? Can I look?" Without waiting for an answer, she tore through a short pile of clothes on the floor and pulled out another burgundy cami, this one a slightly lighter shade.

"I do not understand."

Shelly took her hand. "I can't take the deal, Rumple. You're the singer, not me. But I think there's a way we can both make some money by working together and doing what makes each of us happy. I don't have time to explain it right now. Please trust me."

Rhiannon looked at her for so long without saying anything, Shelly worried she'd say no.

"What do you want me to do?"

She handed her the camisole. "Put this on, no hoodie. And get ready to sing."

* * *

Rhiannon allowed herself to be led up the stairs and into a room filled with humans talking to each other. She walked head down, afraid to see the cruel expressions on their faces. Shelly guided her to a large table and turned to the crowd. A portly man looked at them, his mouth agape.

"Ladies and gentlemen, allow me to re-introduce myself. Larry said that I'm the company's latest talent, but that isn't completely accurate. I'm CEO of Shelly Goodman, Inc. My company will work closely with Temptation Records to develop and market the greatest new talent discovered by A&R. To that end, our client, R.S., will be recording her freshman album immediately." She lifted Rhiannon's hand over her head. "It'll truly be music to move your soul. Now, a sample of what's in store."

Rhiannon stole a glance at Shelly, then at the face of the large man. Shelly's words confused her, but they'd made the man angry. She wanted to get as far away from him as possible, not sing. But Shelly had asked her.

Rhiannon closed her eyes to calm herself and opened them slowly as she began to sing the song that made Shelly cry the first night they'd met. Her friend's warm smile gave her the courage to continue. Other humans looked happy, too. Even the man called Larry no longer fumed. He was clapping for her.

After the song, Shelly introduced her to Larry and several other humans. The one called Bob, who had fathered her friend, pulled her into a hug, kissing the top of her head.

"Not quite what I expected, but I'd say you both are in for the adventure of a lifetime."

After the crowd had dispersed, and she'd feasted on cheese and fruit with Bob, Shelly led her onto a balcony overlooking the city. Rhiannon approached the railing, drawn to the multicolored twinkling lights that made up the cityscape.

"I've never seen the land from up here. It looks so different."

Shelley stood behind her and slipped her arms around her waist. "I imagine lots of things are going to look differently for both of us."

"Does this make you happy?" she asked.

"Yes, very," Shelly assured her. "This is how it was meant to be. Before I forget, I have something to tell you. That night I found you in the basement I heard you singing to Albert."

Rhiannon's heart sank. Shelly would hold power over her.

Shelly kissed her, and murmured against her lips, *"I could beat you at your game, for now I know your one true name."* She added quickly, "But I won't."

Rhiannon pressed her body against Shelly's and kissed her deeply. Now she understood the allure of a happy ending.

Stygian Nights
By Susan Hawes

Look, the problem with immortality is the boredom. I know, you think this god deal must be pretty fabulous. Immense power. Lounging about on clouds. Chucking bolts of lightning at things. Starting wars. Spawning offspring demigods with mortals while disguised as water birds, that sort of thing. The truth? It gets dull. Especially when you're stuck with the worst gig south of Olympus. Way south. As in palace of onyx, endless night, and symphonies of the wailing dead lamenting night and day. After centuries of hanging out with the dead, I had a terminal case of ennui and nothing better to do than watch the human spirits whirlpool around miserably. Occasionally I'd start a fight between my two younger brothers, Boltboy and Tsunamibrains, or make a sly remark in front of their wives about their latest mortal conquest to break myself out of the blahs, but even that was getting old.

I was sulking in one of my few and far between temples when the most amazing thing happened. This curving stunner of a Grecian maiden came hurrying into my temple. Mine! Not Boltboy's, or one of the love goddesses, but mine. I pulled the shadows around me with a sweep of my hand and slid closer to listen to

129

her plea. At first I could barely register what she was asking, because mortals don't ask me for much. Oh, they rage at me when they lose a loved one, or they try to bargain with me when their lives are at risk, but they don't pray to me much. Not like this one. Not that there had ever been anyone else like her. Not even close. I swirled extra shadow around my head as my hair gave a quick flare of excitement and I was afraid the blue light would give me away.

"Please, mighty Hades, Lord of the Dead, God of Wealth, please return my beloved to life. I will do anything if you hear my plea and grant my fervent prayer." She bowed her head, and a long fall of auburn hair slid over her shoulders and screened her face from me. Then she covered her face with her hands and began sobbing.

Well, damn. I wasn't normally empathetic, but something about the sincerity of her tears touched me. She was a far cry from the perfect goddesses above who pouted about their mortal loves passing without a real tear between them. She was genuinely grieving. And gorgeous. Even sobbing her heart out in my temple, she was radiant.

I touched the statue of myself looming over the crying woman and brought it to life. "What would you have of me, mortal?" I rolled my eyes at myself since the Erinyes weren't there to do it. The stuffy formality of interacting with humans normally bored me to death, pun intended, but this one was so far from dull.

"Mighty Hades, show mercy and return my beloved Nikos to me, I beg you. He and I were to marry but his life was cut short. I will bring offerings to your temple every month, whatever pleases you."

She had lifted her face from her hands and was staring up at the statue frowning down on her. Why mortal man persists in carving me as a stern, frowning god I'll never understand.

Even blotchy and swollen from crying, her face was incredibly beautiful. If I'd needed to breathe to live, I might have fainted from lack of air. My chest felt funny as I stared down, admiring her. Her eyes were an incredible shade of amber, so wary and unhappy, but gorgeous. Her hair... I just wanted to wrap my fists in it and bury my face under the weight of it, that wealth of auburn waves.

I gave myself a mental slap for getting distracted. "Not good, imbecile, lusting after the grieving maid asking you to give her lover back," I muttered to myself. "Let's take a peek at his life and hers." Out loud, I boomed at her from my statue self in reply. "Lord Plouton, God of Wealth and Merciful Lord of the Dead, has heard your cries. Return you here in one night's time at the dying of the sun and He shall answer you. Now go!" My statue began to glow bright blue as she rose from her kneeling posture. I gave myself another mental slap as I watched her sway out of my temple. If I'd been a cad like my brothers on Olympus, I'd have already disguised myself as a golden stag or some nonsense and seduced her. But I'd vowed never to be them, flitting from mortal to mortal and leaving a slew of demigods and heartbroken humans in my wake.

I shook myself out of the statue and turned back toward the Underworld. Humans had long forgotten it, but there was a cave that led to my domain under the temple. It was how that annoying shepherd had found his way to demand I give his wife back. But that was ages ago, and nobody had trampled through the asphodel in forever to demand a loved one be returned to them. Until this tall armful of curving beauty had showed up to distract me from boredom.

And plotting my coup.

"Ack!" I pounded a fist against onyx in frustration as I walked through the gates to the underworld. My hair flared a yellowish blue. "I forgot to demand her name. First human to pray to me in I don't know how long and I didn't get her name." I brooded about that as I crossed the fields of asphodel toward my reflecting pool. I lay down next to it and touched the surface of the water with one finger.

"Show me the Nikos she mourns," I said, and slowly moved my finger in a backward arc to see the past. As I lay there watching the man's life run back from the moment of his death, a kernel of anger grew into a leaping bonfire of rage. She mourned him, grieved his passing, even came to pray to me to return him to her and for what? He had lived a wild bacchanal of a life, filled with women who weren't her. And because it was also filled with far too much wine, it was ended under the hooves of oxen as he lurched drunkenly out of a taverna and fell in front of them.

"That glorious flower is crying over this yutz?" I snorted. "Tomorrow night I'll tell her what he was really like and she'll stop mourning him and get a life again."

* * *

Apparently I had greatly underestimated the stubborn faith of the mortal female and the sly deceitfulness of the male. Gorgeous, radiant Alcestis—I had her name now—moved from her postulant kneel and sat her sweetly rounded bottom on my altar.

"What do you mean he isn't deserving of my love?" Her shoulders were squared defiantly, and that dimpled chin of hers angled up at my statue. There were so many parts of her to look at.

Was she kidding me? Had she never noticed him coming home late, or drunk, or rumpled after a night out? I sighed, and it translated through Marble Me as a menacing growl. Oops. I cleared my throat as she jumped up apologetically.

"Lord of the Dead, Keeper of the Underworld, I meant no disrespect." She bowed, and I couldn't stand it another minute.

I pulled my essence from the statue, molded myself into my most human form, and took her hand as I sat on the altar. "Look, Alcestis," I began, then had to stop talking and catch her as she fainted. Oops again. Although shocking her into unconsciousness did allow me to hold her in my arms to keep her from striking that beautiful face on the marble of my altar. And maybe I closed my eyes and rested my cheek on the softness of her hair and found that she smelled like cloves in sunlight. Warm. Sweet. As tempting an armful as she made, I kept my hands to her shoulder and waist just so she wouldn't topple over and get hurt. I have never been like my brothers, and I would not be, not ever.

When she opened those stunning dark, amber eyes again, I tapped her forehead lightly. "Don't faint on me again. I'm tired of the talking through marble thing. I want you to understand what you're asking and make sure it's what you want, because answered prayers don't come cheap." Although if she'd agree to sit here and let me just hold her and drink in the scent of her hair in exchange, I'd probably grant whatever favor she desired.

"You're Hades." The pulse was leaping in her long, slender throat like it was trying to escape her body. "Lord of the Dead." That lovely alabaster complexion of hers had grown alarmingly pale. Shock, I thought, watching her carefully.

"Yes." I cupped her hands between mine and chafed her wrists lightly with my thumbs. I'd seen Heph do it when Aph went all swoony on him.

She blinked up at me, then looked down at my hands curved around hers. "What are you doing to my wrists?"

"Keeping you from fainting again. Don't make me regret talking to you like a person instead of going over all Mighty Marble Me Pronounceth Your Answer." My hair flared up in surprise when she burst out laughing at my answer. From fainting shock to laughing, really, this woman had guts.

"Who knew Lord Hades had a sense of humor?" She smiled and I swear the world exploded into rainbows. Her mouth had the sweetest curve to it, and the dimple in her chin had a twin in her right cheek. I wanted to nuzzle along the dimple and over the line of her jaw to the curve of her long neck and breathe her in.

"You're looking at me very strangely," she said.

"It's a strange situation," I answered. "Not all that often you mortals come flinging yourselves at my altar to ask favors. Even so, when you do, I can't just say sure, I'll bring your loved one back for you. Otherwise there'd be nobody left in the underworld and way too many people up here."

"But I love him." She said it calmly, but her eyes were filling again.

No, no, I wasn't going to let her waste tears on a rat like him, and I hated seeing her so sad. I'd make the bargain so completely unacceptable that there was no way she'd agree, and then she could go about her life and maybe come back to my temple sometimes to thank me. I did a stupid thing once and let a shepherd sway me with the most amazing music, and I gave his wife back to him. But I specified the trust and love between them had to be absolute, and he had to walk all the way out of my domain and into the world of men without looking back even once to be sure she was behind him. Did he manage it? Nope. Even with her life at stake, he just couldn't trust and love enough. This, combined with my brothers' ideas of marriage and fidelity, was why I had no wife or children. Love was like standing on top of a mountain just before a wild goat head butts you off the peak. Beauty followed by a whole lot of pain. No thanks.

"You say you love him, but does he love you?"

She nodded.

"You're sure? How sure are you?"

"He loves me. He promised to marry me." Her words were sure, but her tone wasn't. Not entirely. And her eyes were even less sure, a worried light in them now.

"Would you trade your freedom for his life? You will belong to me if your Nikos turns out to be a roving dog. I'll bring him back for you, but if you're wrong about him and have loved foolishly, you belong to me." There! She'd never go for it. I'd taken a long

135

peek at her life last night too, and she was smart and spirited and warm-hearted.

"Yes, Hades, I will trade. Nikos will never betray me."

I was seething. She deserved better and she was throwing away her soul on a human cur. My hair went bonfire in a flash of rage. "So be it! You have him back, now go."

She was up in an instant and running back toward town. I knew she'd be back, and denied that the tight feeling in my chest was anything other than heartburn.

* * *

I was lounging on the banks of the Styx with Cerberus, watching him chase bones and bring them back to me to throw again. Not very bright for all that he had three heads because sometimes he'd forget which bone I'd thrown and bring back all kinds of wrong things. Charon's pole (he was pissed) once, a big rock in one of his other mouths another time...you'd think I'd have learned after the time he dropped Prometheus' liver in my lap. Gross. Even the god of death doesn't like organs torn from the living.

My dull day was interrupted without warning by an angry scream emanating from my temple. I tossed a whole set of rib bones to Cerberus to keep him busy and walked into the portal leading to my temple.

If I had thought Alcestis was beautiful in mourning, she was glorious in anger. The very tips of her hair vibrated as she paced back and forth at my altar. I stood back to watch as she cursed, cried, screamed, and vented. I couldn't keep my eyes off the rolling sway of her hips as she moved or the furious light in her lovely eyes. She was amazing.

"So." I molded myself into a human form and sat on the altar, still watching her storm back and forth. "Hello, Alcestis."

"Hello? Hello, yes, right, it's Lord Hades the inscrutable. So you were right, and I'm stupid. And you could have just said 'no, Allie, Nikos is a cheating lying mongrel and he's slept with every woman in town' but no!'"

I was stunned. "Hey, I made the bargain so horrible I assumed there was no way you were going to sacrifice yourself for him."

She turned, hand on one deeply curved hip, eyes flashing. "That's what love is, Hades. Sacrificing yourself for your love."

I shook my head. "You don't get it. Even now. Sit."

She threw me a glare and paced away.

"Oh no, sweet Alcestis, you don't get to do that now." I flung out one hand and pointed at her ankle. A delicate gold bracelet appeared there, gleaming.

Stiffly, unwillingly, she walked slowly back to me. I was amazed again at her strength. Most mortal women would have already broken under the compulsion chain around that lovely leg. The gold glowed softly with the magic of her bargain, her own willing surrender to me. She couldn't disobey me or deny me and yet she struggled against the anklet to walk at her own pace, and kept herself upright even though I'd told her to sit.

I sighed. "Alcestis, please. Just sit and let's talk. You're angry because you traded your soul for the boytoy and he turned out to be an ass. You now know he wasn't worthy of your sacrifice."

"You couldn't have just said that at the beginning?" she burst, her cheeks flushed with anger. "Oh, no, you ask me if I'm sure but can't be bothered to give me all the information I needed! Isn't that just like a man. God or mortal, that's a man for you. Don't bother communicating," she continued.

I was too fascinated watching the hectic flush in her throat and cheeks heighten to argue. Was she right? I thought I'd discouraged her from throwing her life away for someone who didn't truly love her, not like I....

Dammit. No. Hades doesn't fall in love. Not with mortals, or playful nymphs, or even goddesses. I had a revenge to plot, Olympus to overthrow, Titans to free, and a demi-god to get out of my way before I could do any of it. I did not have time to fall in love with a smart, strong, beautiful woman who'd chosen really badly.

I gestured at the anklet. "Alcestis, we'll talk about this at home."

"Home?" She looked around the temple a little wildly. "I can't live here."

I laughed. "No. I meant my home." I closed my fingers gently around her wrist and transported us to my porch with the view of the ugly river and the uglier boat.

* * *

Several months later

"Alcestis?" I called her name uncertainly from the front porch. Agamemnon and Achilles had been at it again in the Elysian Fields, their war games spilling blood over the grass.

"Returned from the wars?" Her cheeky grin

greeted me at the doorway. "Hermes is in the other room for you. Must be important."

"It's always important up there," I grumbled, extending a hand to her. "Did you get Nessus to agree to support me?"

She rolled her eyes at me. "Would I dare disobey a direct order from you, oh mighty Lord of the Dead?"

"Quit that," I muttered as she slipped her hand into mine. My fascination with the softness of her skin had only increased over time and my thumb ached to caress her in the brief press of our hands. I wanted to pull her closer and lay my face on her hair and just hold her, but never did because she gave no indication she'd welcome that.

She swung my arm a bit as we walked. "Achilles came by while you were wooing Agamemnon back to peaceable ways of thinking."

I growled. "What did he want? To re-enact the battle of Troy in the Asphodel Fields?" Pretty, smooth Achilles had been here alone with Alcestis? My stomach hurt.

"He came to apologize for inciting Agamemnon to riot," she said calmly. "Your hair is singeing the paintings. What has you so upset? The Greeks and Trojans cleaned up the mess and nobody can really die again down here, so what's the harm? They're warriors and they like fighting. It's stupid, but that's men for you."

My mouth was open. "To apologize?" I paused, my flaming hair settling to a smolder in surprise.

"Yes. He knows you get irritated with the noise and smoke and intestines all over the place when they have battles."

"How exactly did he come to know that?" I

followed her into the kitchen where Hermes lounged, winged sandals fluttering impatiently on the table. "And you, get your feet off there. Flying or not, they're still feet, and I don't want them up where I eat."

"You're a god," Hermes said lazily. "Quit fussing about where my feet are. You're commanded to a party in honor of The Big Guy's youngest offspring coming of age."

I stopped again. "Coming of age? I thought the little tyke had vanished ages ago." My heart lurched. The Fates had told me that if the hero fought at his father's side, the Titans would fail and my little rebellion would crash and burn. My Furies were supposed to have fed him a potion, stolen his immortality, and rendered him useless in the fight.

Hermes grinned. "They thought so too, but he's been raised by mortals and is currently slaying monsters all over Greece. At this rate, he's bound to get his godhood back."

I concentrated on my breathing and not letting my hair burst into a giant bonfire of rage. Slaying monsters. The very monsters I needed to distract the gods so I could release the Titans when the planets aligned. The one person who could stop my hostile takeover. I gritted my teeth. "Lovely. I'll be there."

"And your date?" Hermes' grin told me he hadn't missed the gorgeous woman pouring a goblet of ambrosia for herself.

"My concern," I replied. "Tell my younger brother we'll be thrilled to visit and celebrate with him."

As soon as Hermes had fluttered off, I let my seething rage explode in a cone of flame high enough to reach the ceiling. "He's alive? ERINYES!"

140

As I hollered their name, the Furies burst into being in the kitchen. Alcestis sighed. "Hades, you've smudged the marble again. Try to control your temper. I'll have to call Ajax over tomorrow to get it clean again. Even Achilles isn't tall enough to reach it. What's the big deal if your brother's son turns 18?"

"Because all those monsters you've been helping me negotiate with are supposed to be supporting me when I overthrow Olympus." The Furies were watching with fascination from the corner of the kitchen where they'd taken refuge. "Which won't work as long as that little jolt of static off the ol' lightning bolt is still a demigod! You said he was taken care of!" I rounded on the Erinyes with a glare.

"He was," Fury One offered. "Mostly."

"Mostly!" I was furious, but one look at Alcestis distracted me enough to keep my hair from flaring up and getting more soot on the ceiling.

"Overthrowing Olympus," Alcestis said thoughtfully.

"I have every right," I said hotly. "Those two tricked me into taking the Underworld. I'm just going to take back the kingdom I should have had in the first place. And I can't do it if that hero is at his father's side."

"He's mostly not a god," Fury Two muttered. "It's not our fault he didn't drink the whole potion."

"Mostly," I repeated, still furious. "And the three of you," I stopped suddenly as I wheeled around to face them again and they vanished. Alcestis stood there, tapping one delicate foot against the marble floor.

"You're being unreasonable." She picked up her goblet of ambrosia and walked out to the front porch.

I followed, irritated. "I'm being unreasonable? Because my minions can't even handle a simple mission to steal the immortality of a demigod, or because Greek warriors insist on hanging around my palace all damn day when I'm off trying to keep the underworld from exploding into battle and keep Cerberus from chewing the front gates, or because my two younger brothers tricked me into ruling the worst place in Greece, or..." I sat down next to her as she leaned back, curling comfortably into the soft fluffy cushions I'd woven for her out of asphodel and shadows.

"Why do you think this is the worst place in Greece?" Her eyes met mine as she took another sip. As she pulled the goblet away again, the drop of ambrosia clinging to her full lower lip tempted me unbearably. I wanted so badly to lean toward her and lick it from her beautiful mouth, to taste the nectar of the gods mixed with the flavor of her lips. I fought down a tremor of desire and gritted my teeth.

"Look at it! A river full of dead people, an ugly boat and a cheerless bony ferryman going back and forth night and day. A whole field of nothing but white flowers, dead Greek heroes re-fighting battles every minute, a palace of black marble and onyx, no sun..."

"You're the Lord of the Underworld, aren't you?" Her calm was beginning to irritate me. The pliant obedient slave I'd thought I'd get when her bargain for Nikos' life was nothing of the sort. She argued with me, never cleaned the palace, asked impertinent questions, played fetch with Cerberus, danced with centaurs, and was generally a saucy, willful woman.

"Yes, Alcestis, I am Lord of the Underworld." I answered her calmly in kind. "And, what?"

"So you determine how things look, don't you. Whether Charon is bony and morose or a cheerful lecherous brat like Achilles. Whether his boat is ugly or woven of asphodels. Which, by the way, are gorgeous. And Helios doesn't drive the sun through for us, but your hair gives a lovely blue glow to this beautiful palace all the time."

My mouth had dropped open as I listened to her. "You like it here?"

She nodded and sat up a bit, sliding her feet into my lap before curling up again. "I love the sound of the river when we sit out here talking. Charon knows some wicked jokes when he's not being what he thinks you want him to be. I love the asphodels turning blue when you walk through them and lend them your glow. I love sipping ambrosia with you while Ajax and Achilles wrestle in the field. I love listening to Orpheus sing to us while I'm painting and watching you smile when you think I'm not paying attention. I love the soft cushions you scattered all over the palace because you worry I'm not comfortable sitting on marble."

I couldn't speak. Something tight and hot was searing through my chest. My hair had faded to a soft blue fire in my astonishment.

She sat up, my Alcestis, and slid the rest of her way into my lap. Her small hands moved from her lap to cradle my cheeks and my heart stopped beating for a long moment.

"Alcestis?" My throat was too tight to speak. My voice was hoarse, barely a whisper.

"Hades," she smiled. "And if you aren't the most honorable god, I'll eat the gold filigree off the chandeliers. I fell in love with empty words once and traded my soul for his life. But I can't complain because it brought me to the palace of a beautiful, moody god who would bribe Hermes to deliver my favorite foods, who would track down a spider goddess to weave me beautiful clothes, who would make cushions for my comfort out of the darkness of his home. That moment of stupidity brought me to you. When your brothers run around ravishing nymphs disguised as swans, you never tried to even kiss me, and I've been living under your roof as your slave."

I swallowed, or tried to. I couldn't talk, so I nodded.

"I was swayed by words, my Hades, but you have swayed me with actions." She leaned up and touched her lips lightly to mine.

I trembled once and lost my sanity in her eyes. I crushed her to me and devoured that delicious, clever mouth with lips and tongue and teeth. I kissed her until I couldn't breathe and her heart was thudding against my hands when they cupped the soft heaviness of her breasts. I licked the taste of nectar from her tongue as my fingers worshipped the sweet dimpling of her knees and thighs. I suckled the softness of her skin at the back of her shoulder, the nape of her neck, the long line of her throat. I was rigid, shaking with yearning, and yet I held back even as she cried out for me, begging me sweetly to take her as I laid her back on the cushion and pushed her gown out of my way. I swept my tongue over the soft protrusion of her belly and lower, burying my face in her curls and inhaling the sweet perfume of her need. She called out for me again as I pressed her thighs wider, feeling them tremble in my hands. My thumbs opened her for me, and I pushed my tongue high inside her, plunging it deeper as her words turned to moaning cries. When her hips twitched restlessly back and forth and I heard the breath catch and stop in her throat, I thrust two fingers into her hard and suckled at the swollen pearl between her legs. She screamed for me then, arching up against my mouth over and over, and I drank her down. Every sweet salty drop of her liquid pleasure coating my face was a feast, and I gobbled and licked and laved, ravenous even as I sated her.

I slid up her body, kissing and nibbling at her soft, full breasts and taking the pushed up gown higher, until I lifted her limp body and pulled it off completely. There. Laid against my cushions, the tangle of her hair red and wild and spread over the couch, her eyes unfocused and glazed. Her soft round cheeks bright, red, and damp with sweat, that long beautiful throat struggling over each uneven breath. She was glorious. My saucy, bright, beautiful Allie.

And I was on fire to be inside her. "Alcestis," I whispered, burying my face in the curve of her throat. "I love you." And on the last syllable, I drove into her.

Her eyes flew open again, fixed wildly on mine. She cried out and I felt her stretch and ripple around me as I plunged deeper, pulled back, and took her deeper still. She was panting again as my balls slapped against her with each thrust. I circled my hips, angling to catch her sensitive flesh, and felt her seize up around me again. Her breath sobbed out unevenly and her fingers clutched at me.

I whispered it again and again as I stroked into her faster. Her head jerked to the side and her hips slammed up against me. Her whole body arched up to meet mine over and over, and she let out an ululating cry of triumph, writhing in my arms and driving me to completion. I exploded inside her, pleasure peaking so hard and hot it was nearly painful.

I turned her to her side, not wanting to crush her. I brushed tears from her cheek and followed them with nuzzling kisses, holding her to me as I softened inside her. The glorious heat between us trickled to a slow smolder. Her heart slowed in tandem with mine, and her eyes opened halfway, heavy-lidded.

I waited for the smile in her eyes to reach her lips, and kissed her tenderly to coax it from her. My hand curled to cup one breast gently and I leaned down to lick beaded sweat from her neck. Every liquor of her body was intoxicating.

"You love me," she whispered. "That's all I want. Just you."

"I want to give you more," I murmured, nuzzling kisses over her throat.

Her hands brought my face up to hers, insistent. "This is all we need, Hades, my love. Just us. Just this. We are enough as long as we're together."

I traced the curve of her smile with a fingertip. "You are enough, my Allie. Always."

"I should hope so," she smiled. "I turned down six warriors and three kings for you." Her teasing grin made me laugh and I hugged her to me.

"Which ones, so I can kill them?" That made her laugh and she snuggled closer, nestling in my arms like she belonged there. Which she did, and always had.

"Not important," she yawned. "They're all Greek to me. Thank you, my love, for showing me that words and promises aren't love. You told me loving isn't sacrificing yourself for the other. You were right. Love is you."

"The god of death is love?" I teased her as she rubbed her cheek against my shoulder.

"In your case, my love, absolutely. Now hush and hold me. I want to sleep in your arms a bit before we try that again."

I laughed and held my Alcestis closer, hers as she was mine, at last.

Kink Midas
By Barbra Campbell

Midas

I leaned against the doorway unable to tear my eyes from Goldie's bare legs and ass. The scant purple strip of thong didn't cover much and her T-shirt rode up her cheeks as she bent over, concerned with something on the bookshelf.

She'd only been my live-in housekeeper for three days, but I'd grown attached to her attentiveness, confidence, and sweet smile I sensed wasn't quite genuine. My core stirred with the desire to fix that.

Something had her full attention and she hadn't noticed me.

This was the first time I'd caught her roaming the house at night. Also the first time I'd seen her in what must be her pajamas, or lack thereof. "Keep sticking your ass out and I'm liable to smack it, Goldie."

Startled, she bumped her head on the bookshelf as she stood too quickly. Facing me, one hand darted behind her back holding something and the other rubbed the sore spot on her head. A torturous pout formed on her lips. "That won't do either of us any good, will it?"

I wanted to comfort her. I wanted to do a lot of things to her. Her sass fueled my spirit as much as her

148

body fueled my need. My breaths were heavy as I tried to pull my mind out of the useless gutter. One smack of her ass and she'd be another golden statue to stick in my garden. I tore my eyes from her lips but they trailed downward, noticing her shirt had ridden up while she rubbed her head.

A slightly larger patch of purple fabric covered what I could only imagine was a pussy as sweet as the rest of her. My dick ached to be inside a woman again. Yet another simple pleasure I could no longer enjoy.

She cleared her throat and dropped her hand, pulling the fabric of her T-shirt down.

I didn't care that she saw me staring at her hungrily. Common knowledge had me pegged as a greedy bastard. Everyone hated me. I was shocked she'd even replied to my ad for a housekeeper. Trailing my eyes upward, ready for her to tell me what an ass I was, her tits held my gaze.

She'd yanked the T-shirt down causing it to pull tight against her ample breasts. Her perky nipples begged me to touch them.

My mouth watered and my lips parted, betraying my thoughts. I clenched my fists, frustration consuming me. One god damn touch and I'd ruin it. A guy could only stay celibate so long.

"Hey, up here," she said and wrapped her other arm over her breasts. A bag hung from her hand and she fidgeted nervously when my eyes dropped to it.

"I see housekeeping isn't your only skill, you little thief." I pushed off the doorway and headed to my bedroom.

"I'm sorry, King Midas." She rushed toward me,

extending a hand, then apparently thinking better of it as she stilled herself inches from my arm.

Both of us froze. She had every right to be worried…certain death for her if we touched. But I craved her touch more than I'd craved anything. I stared at her fingers, slender with beautiful nails painted gold. Had she chosen that for me? No one did anything for me. My chest tightened and I fought the urge to take her hand in mine. I exhaled sharply.

Imagining the softness of her skin, the tenderness of her touch, and the rake of her nails down my back, anguish racked my core. The simplest acts had been taken from me by a drunken wish. That bastard Dionysus would pay.

"Take it all. It doesn't mean anything to me," I growled and continued to my room.

"Wait." Her footsteps padded on the floor behind me.

I stopped, ground my teeth, and faced her with fire in my soul. "What's the point of running background checks? Your record was clean, and here you are stealing." I reached for the bag and she jerked away, stumbling backward, her face turning ashen.

She held a hand up and tears rolled down her cheeks. "I'm sorry, King. I had my record cleaned. Please don't be mad. I'll put everything back." Her shoulders sagged as she set the bag on the shelf.

"So you are a thief. And a clever one." My curiosity peaked.

Facing away, her head hung low. "I am. But I'm not clever enough. I keep getting caught. That's why I had to get my record cleaned. I grew up poor, not enough food on the table most days. I didn't finish school because the kids teased me about my ratty clothes. I don't have any skills. No one wants to hire a high school dropout which means I stay poor. I guess that made me love money so I steal. People say money can't buy happiness, but it can. But that's not the only reason I applied for the job."

Her voice was almost inaudible on her last statement and I wanted to believe her sincerity.

Chances were she was scamming me. Wouldn't be the first. But something was different about Goldie. She resurrected feelings I'd considered dead. My heart stirred in her presence, along with other parts. Why did I even toy with the idea of touching her? Why couldn't I fight back the urge to wrap my arms around her? Why did I entertain the notion deep in my soul to make love to Goldie?

She walked back to the bookshelf and unloaded the golden rose petals she'd collected.

I should have let her go before I did something I'd regret. I'd tried to have sex. Thought I was clever figuring out condoms were like my clothes and didn't turn to gold, but one wrong move and my dick had been caught in a golden vise. Not something I wanted to experience again.

"You can take whatever you want if you'll tell me how you got your record cleared."

Wiping the tears from her cheeks, she faced me. "Don't think poorly of me. I really am a good person, most of the time. I found this lawyer. He has a way of making problems go away. Maybe he could help you."

Her downcast eyes and soft guilty tone drove me crazy, not to mention she admitted she loved money. A woman after my own heart. We all had our reasons for our actions, and it didn't make us bad people.

"He could make *my* problem go away?" My problem wasn't as simple as thievery. I'd been fooled by a god, demigod, whatever the fuck he was. The way Dionysus told the story, he asked me to think about my wish, which was true. What he failed to mention was that I was under the influence of his beloved wine, eliminating any chance of making a wise choice.

"I can give you his number," she offered.

"I don't have a phone."

"Right. I'll text him about you. And just to be clear...by your problem, you're referring to the Golden Touch?"

"Yeah."

"But you have it made. You'll never run out of money," she said not understanding the full complications.

"It's not enough." I stormed to my room eager to get away from her allure.

* * *

Goldie

I couldn't blame Midas if he saw me as nothing other than a cheap thief. My initial intent in applying to work for him was to steal. Then I met him. A beast of a man who seduced me with his mere presence. Initially I'd thought it was his wealth but we were kindred spirits.

Every glance at him left me wanting, craving his touch. The pain he suffered was unjust but I applauded him for moving forward without complaint.

If I couldn't get my lawyer, Hadley, to help him, I suspected I'd be fired. In the three days I'd worked for Midas, his kindness and regret had shown through.

Millions of people, including me, loved money. Why did he have to pay such a steep price? More proof that life wasn't fair. Damn gods had too much fun meddling in human lives. Give them a chance and they'd vilify you.

I pitied the King. Slipping on my yoga pants, a long sleeve shirt, and gloves, I was going through with my gamble. Worst case, I wouldn't have to worry about anything ever again. Word had it the transformation to gold was instant, no time to experience any pain.

Walking down the dark hallway, I pushed Midas' door open and slipped into his room. Deep, paced breathing assured me he remained asleep. I gave my eyes a second to adjust to the darkness and looked in the direction of his breaths.

My courage was bolstered by the possibility my lawyer could help. Midas couldn't tell me to hit the road quite yet.

As the darkness morphed into vague forms then outlines of furniture, I made my way to his bed and sat on the edge.

I was surprised to find his bedding hadn't turned to gold. Thankful. Dionysus wasn't a total ass.

Fear sparked through me then morphed into elation as I gently set my hand on his covered arm. I remained a living, breathing human. For a few seconds I absorbed Midas' heat, followed the slight sway of his body with his breaths, wished I could crawl under the covers and hold him.

My heart broke. His last comment about money not being enough had torn me apart. He'd learned his lesson. I dropped my head back, silently cursing the gods.

Trailing my hand down the curves of his arm, I craved running my fingers over his muscled body. Lifting weights was one of the few things he could do to pass the time without repercussions. Thankfully one of his previous staff had helped him figure out how to eat, otherwise he would have withered away instead of sculpting himself to this god-like perfection.

"What the fuck?" He bolted up right and slung himself to the edge of the bed, away from me.

He continued through heavy breaths. "You touched me? How? Do you have a death wish?"

"I only touched the covers."

"Are you sure? Your fingers, I felt them...so real..." His words hung in the room. I wanted him to say more, admit his attraction to me. I'd seen it in the way his eyes lingered, but I'd also seen his frustration.

"Have you been with a woman since the wish?"

"You're paid to keep house not ask questions. Go back to sleep."

I curled myself into a ball on the empty side of the bed, on top of the covers, making a spectacle of fluffing the pillow to get it just right.

"What the hell are you doing?" He was standing and his voice raised, sounding defensive.

"Going back to sleep," I said as nonchalantly as possible.

"You can't sleep in my bed. I'll kill you."

"I came prepared: gloves, long sleeves, yoga pants, socks. The only thing at risk is my face. Don't try to kiss me."

"Not all I want to do," he mumbled and sat on the edge of the bed. "Go back to your own room."

That mumble was all the encouragement I

needed. I reached for his shoulder, hesitating as I considered what pose I'd be immortalized in if this went wrong. Shifting to my knees, I positioned myself directly behind him and reached for both shoulders.

He flinched but not enough to pull away. All good.

I worked my fingers over his broad shoulders, kneading his muscles, noticeably releasing his tension. His body was hard, the way I liked my men. He was rich. He was single. And I was almost desperately attracted to him. My ideal man, almost. I had to make it work.

He groaned as my gloved hands traced over his back. His head rolled side to side.

"You like that?"

"Fuck, yeah, but why risk your life?"

"I need you." I whispered the words to keep the seduction going.

"No, nobody needs my curse."

'That's exactly what I need. I love money. I love danger. I—"

"Stop. I've heard this before. It didn't work out." He leaned forward to get up but I tugged on his shoulders to keep him sitting.

Leaning in, I ran my hands over him, down his chest, and pressed my body against him, making sure to keep my face away to the side.

The long, slow inhale and exhale assured me I was breaking him down.

"The gods fucked my parents," I told him. "Apparently, my mother declined Apollo's advances because she was married. The gods don't take well to being turned down as you can imagine. Dionysus

155

owed his brother a favor so they came up with a plan. Dionysus cursed my father to be a grape farmer which sounded like a blessing until Apollo cursed my mother with plague. I guess it was supposed to tear my parents apart but they stayed together at the expense of poverty."

"And the curse continues with you stealing from me then rubbing your tits into my back. If you understand the pain of the gods' folly, why torture me?"

"When my father couldn't farm because of my mother's plague, I learned to steal to put food on the table. I'm addicted to money, gambling. I have debts. I thought your Golden Touch was a dream."

"A nightmare. Take everything. What do I care?"

"I see that now. You've moped around the house, everyone's afraid of you, and you're afraid of what you might do to them."

"And yet, here you are giving me a useless hard-on."

"Why let me touch you, then?"

He jumped up and my face nearly crashed in to his back as I fell forward. His words were angry and gravelly. "Do I have to say it? Do I have to admit I was wrong? There are better things in life than money."

He stormed around the bed toward the door, my heart breaking for the man whose life was ruined by one simple wish.

Anger flowed through me and I scampered off the bed, grabbing Midas' arm. "Don't let those fuckers win."

"They're the gods."

"So let's knock them off their clouds." If either of

us could turn our life around, it would be a slap in the face to the gods.

"You're cute when you're mad."

I rubbed my hand over his cock, bringing him erect and my breath hitched at his size. Perhaps the worst case of blue balls in history, and this guy was holding out. "There's nothing cute about how mad I am. Let's prove them wrong. Your clothes, your sheets…not everything turns to gold, I'm guessing condoms don't. They're kind of like clothes."

"Condoms aren't the problem. If anything goes wrong, I'm a killer and my dick's stuck in a statue. Trust me, not good for either of us. Not all of my statues are appropriate for the garden."

His dick twitched under my hand and his hot breath trailed over my face. He rubbed his hands through his hair. I ran my free hand over his chest, the contours of his muscles making my knees week. "I have an idea."

"No," he said definitively but I ignored him.

I kissed my gloved fingertip and placed it on his lips. He closed his eyes and dropped his head back.

"Don't go anywhere," I said and dashed to my room to grab my handcuffs. They'd become a staple since my break-ins sometimes went wrong.

When I rushed back into his room, I flipped the light on and caught sight of his hand gripping his erection through his sleep pants. My eyes had to have bulged out of my head. His hand around his shaft was the hottest thing ever. My desire to be with Midas wasn't developing slowly and beautifully, it was instant and carnal.

I set the cuffs on the nightstand. "Plan B."

"What happened to Plan A?"

"Later." I disrobed.

He eyed the cuffs curiously, then held my gaze. No more stolen glances. He stared at me with the intensity of a man who hadn't been with a woman in a long time. "We can't."

I sat on the bed, leaned against the headboard, and spread my legs. "I'm going to get myself off, and you're going to do the same for yourself."

His gaze dropped to my pussy. "Why aren't you afraid of me?"

"I have nothing to lose." Grabbing one of my breasts, I worked the flesh and pinched my nipple. Slipping a finger of my free hand in my mouth, I slowly drew it out and slid my hand between my legs.

He gulped.

"I hope I don't have to do this alone," I said to encourage him.

Shucking his clothes as fast as he could, he stumbled and caught himself before crashing onto the bed as I lurched to the side. Close call.

He fisted his erection, pumping it, groaning. His lidded eyes fixed on my fingers as I toyed with my clit and sank them into my wetness. He whispered, "You smell so sweet."

I pulled my fingers to my mouth and licked them. "I taste sweet too. It's all for you and that rock-hard cock I wish I could put my mouth on."

"Shit, tell me what you want." The need in his voice escalated the electricity sparking through me.

I dipped my fingers back to my clit driving my pleasure to new heights. Between ragged breaths, I said, "I really want it in here, stretching me. It would

158

feel so good, but I need to see you come. Can you shoot your load on me or will it kill me?"

"Fuck." He stopped pumping, closed his eyes, and took a deep breath before continuing. "It won't kill you."

I didn't care how he knew. I licked my lips ready to taste the salty essence of my King. "Then spray it all over me."

Midas stepped closer to the bed and stroked his shaft. His eyes raked over my body and the feral look in them pushed me over the edge.

I writhed and moaned as I watched his thigh muscles flex, his jaw clench, and his cock strain. "I'm coming."

His eyes left my body as his head dropped back and he groaned, "Goldie."

I'd fantasized his cum would be golden, but no such luck. The warm, white streams shot from his cock, hitting my face, tits, and mound. I worked his slick cum into mine as I milked myself for every last ounce of pleasure. My own flurry of orgasm pulled my eyes shut and I forced them back open to watch his bicep drive his hand and force more cum onto me.

He draped his hand over his semi-hard cock as he finished. "Fuck, Goldie, you're incredible."

Spent, but aching for the thrust of his cock inside of me, I licked his cum from my lips and spread it over my breasts. "Next time, you have to be inside of me."

"It's too risky." His cock strained under his hand betraying his words. He went into the master bathroom and came back with a washcloth for me.

I wiped off then extended the handcuffs and pulled my clothes on. "I have to have you. Put your clothes back on. And I need scissors."

"What? Why?" He took the cuffs, careful not to touch the exposed skin of my hand since I hadn't put my gloves on yet. We were a mere inch apart. An inch that was everything I wanted but would ruin everything.

"I need to feel your stiff cock. We can do this. If we're fully clothed and you wear a condom, and cuff me to the bed. We can make this work." I heard the desperation in my own voice and willed Midas to trust me.

"I don't want to hurt you, little thief. I'll give you everything. You don't have to have sex with me."

I picked up his clothes and thrust them at him. My lack of close relationships left me short on words to express what I was feeling. "I came here because I fell in love with your money, but it's become more."

"Sex? To spite the gods? Is that any better?" He carefully took his clothes and walked out of the room.

The loss consuming me was unbearable. Was it just sex for him? I'd never wanted something as badly as I wanted to be his queen, but it wasn't for the gold. It was for the man. His departure ripped my heart from my chest. I couldn't live without him. Now to convince him he *could* live with me.

He rounded the corner dressed, and I dropped my head in my hands.

"Don't deny me the chance to be with you," I begged.

A shiny glimmer caught my peripheral vision. Scissors. My heart raced.

He smiled and shook his head. "You make me weak. I don't want to turn you to gold, but I can't bear seeing you unhappy."

I took the scissors and went back to the room,

getting on the bed. Spreading my legs, I pulled the fabric of my yoga pants out so I wouldn't cut myself and snipped a hole.

"That's not very big," he said questioningly, his face flushing.

"Small on the safe side, the fabric will stretch." I winked.

"What if you break me and I try to kiss you?" He pulled a condom out of the drawer.

"You won't be able to." I knelt on the bed facing the headboard and placed my hands on it. "You're going to cuff me to the headboard and take me from behind."

"You're so fucking clever, but really, you don't have to prove anything. I already love...your cleverness. I love your cleverness." The light blush that had colored his cheeks brightened, and he wouldn't meet my gaze as I looked at him over my shoulder.

My heart soared as I caught his slip. People had been nothing more than obstacles to me, means to an end. Midas touched something in me. He'd turned my black heart to a heart of gold, and I wanted to give him the world.

With my long sleeves tucked into my gloves, my skin was secure and Midas brought the handcuffs to them. "Are you sure?"

"Did you notice how wet I am?"

"I don't want you to do this for the wrong reasons."

I fought back my words. I'd never been close to anyone. The struggles of my childhood meant I didn't know how to bond. I wasn't sure how to be vulnerable, but with him I was willing to try. "My reasons are pure. I want this."

He clasped the handcuff around one wrist and then the other, securing my hands to the headboard and allowing me to support myself on my elbows, keeping the exposed skin of my face away from him. Ass in the air.

The rip of the condom package might as well have lit a fire to my already burning need.

The few seconds he took to sheath himself passed like an eternity.

His tip prodded at my entrance and his hands gripped my hips. "Goldie, I love you."

The words barely escaped his lips when he thrust into me, stretching and pounding with such force my body rocked back and forth. All the lust I'd seen in his eyes funneled itself into what I prayed wouldn't be the death of me.

My body raced toward orgasm. The scent of his cum lingering from earlier, his firm grip, every slam of his hips into my ass, and my submissive position, exposed and needy, the entire scene intoxicated me, dizziness taking over as I savored our contact.

His hand loosened on my hip and he smacked my butt. "You have the best ass. I've wanted to ride you from the moment you interviewed." He nearly growled his words out.

"Again." The thrill, the life, that surged from his hand to my cheek when he spanked me made my pussy clamp around his length.

"You're mine. No one else can have you." His words wound their way through my heart and soul.

No one wanted me. No one trusted me. "I'm yours." The words spilled out of me as I attempted to hold off my orgasm, but another smack to my ass and I spiraled out of control. My body convulsing as his cock swelled and he thrust a hand over my shoulder.

I jerked my head to the opposite side, resisting the temptation to kiss him, the need to have my skin against his.

He pulled his hand back immediately and gripped my waist, crashing my body into his as we climaxed together. Our bodies gave everything we could, and I was still alive. He slid himself out and collapsed next to me as I lowered myself to the bed.

Midas reached for the key.

"Don't. I won't be able to stop myself from touching you," I said.

He ran a hand over my back and trailed kisses over my clothes.

I drifted to sleep with nearly every part of my being fulfilled.

* * *

Midas

I locked myself in my room, avoiding Goldie for two days. She left trays of food but I didn't open the door to get them. My guilt over risking her life was unbearable. If we continued our romps, we'd have a far worse accident than a pregnancy.

A knock.

"Don't you get it? I'm too dangerous for you. The only way I can resist you is to stay locked away."

"You'll die if you don't eat," she said through the door.

"Take whatever you need for money and never come back." I don't know how or why my heart opened to her, but it had. Now all I could do was protect her. I needed her to believe I would die if she didn't leave, it was my only hope. Truth be known, I was a junk food addict and had a stash in my room. Not the healthiest way to live for a couple of days, but I was fine.

"Will you eat if I leave?"

"How can I ever be sure you're gone? I'd rather die than kill you." The truth.

That's how our conversations went through the locked door.

Another knock, not long after the last one. "I told you to leave."

"Hadley got back to me. Dionysus has been under attack for getting humans drunk before using his godly wiles on them. I guess his celestial peers are ridiculing him for it, kind of a sound mind and body breach of contract thing. He's willing to compromise rather than have it brought to public attention that you, one of his most famous cases, was drunk when you made your foolish wish. He can play off the change as having taught humans a lesson and as a show of mercy." Her words rushed out in a flurry of excitement.

I stood behind the door, afraid to let hope surge through me. "How well do you know Hadley? Can he pull this off?"

"I'm holding the offer in my hands, written by Dionysus' own pen. He listed three options. You just have to pick which one you'd prefer."

"Slide it under the door."

"Nope."

"Read it to me."

"Nope, you'll have to open up."

Could be a scam. She didn't let ethics get in the way. "How can I be sure you're not lying?"

"You have to trust me."

I wasn't sure how good of a faker she was but her words had been enthusiastic when she explained the scenario. I wanted to trust her. I wanted to see her again. Needed to. But I promised myself not to have sex with her again until I was sure my curse was over. The offer reeked of being too good to be true. My desire to be near her, see her smile, and be together overrode my hesitation.

"Are you covered? I'm going to open the door. I don't want to touch you...well, I do, so make sure you're covered."

"I am."

Opening the door, my hands trembled at her cautious smile. Beautiful and misunderstood. I wanted to make the world right for her. My entire body ached for unfiltered contact. I braced my hands on either side of the doorframe to keep from reaching out or moving toward her. "Hold it up."

She held the paper and I read.

Being of sound mind and body, and not intoxicated, I could continue my Golden Touch, I could regain my ability to touch things, but not people, or I could resign myself to the life of a grape farmer.

The glow of Dionysus' signature led me to think it was authentic. In typical deity deceptiveness, there wasn't much of a choice.

Goldie fidgeted while I read. "King, this is it. Your curse can be lifted. And he sent this special pen so you won't turn it to gold."

How was she optimistic? "And be a farmer? Like your father? He's pitting us against each other, playing you against your past."

"I'll take my chances. Otherwise, we both know you'll kill me."

An unbreakable spirit. In our short time together, she hadn't taken crap from me and I suspected she didn't take it from anyone else, apparently even the gods. I reached for the paper but she pulled away.

"Wait. There's one other thing," she said.

"What?"

"Meet me in the dining room." She rushed off before I had a chance to object.

How could she dangle freedom in front of me then tell me to wait? I stepped back into my room and slipped a shirt on.

"Okay," she called from the other room. The lightness in her voice was tinged with a hint of guilt.

Rounding the corner, I saw rocks all over the floor in front of her. Giving her a questioning glance, I walked closer.

"Before you give up your powers, I need a favor." She'd never been sheepish, but there she was wringing her hands and down casting her eyes.

"You want me to turn these rocks to gold?" Disbelief tinged my words. Had she learned nothing from my suffering? I surveyed the shelves full of golden items and rubbed my forehead. I'd been used. Foolish to believe anyone could love me for myself. I studied her and she met my gaze from under her lashes.

I called over my shoulder as I left the room. "I already told you to take anything and everything. Don't be greedy."

"There's only one thing of yours I want."

"My Touch, yada yada…"

"No."

Mumbled curses met my ears as it sounded like she was walking through the rocks she's spread on the floor.

I turned in time to find her standing a foot behind me, stopping short as I quit walking. "What part of 'take it all' do you not understand? Just leave me out of it."

Her hand stilled in mid-air between us. Tears formed in her eyes. "The only thing I want is your heart. You said you loved me. It was in the throes of passion but better than anyone else has ever said. No one has ever made me feel the way you do."

We stared into each other's eyes, my heart begging to belong to her, but afraid it wasn't ready to trust again.

"The rocks?" I asked.

Her shoulders slunk and she stepped back to them. "My debt. If you'll turn these rocks to gold, I can pay my debts."

"Why not just take any of this?" I waved my hand at the shelves.

"These are your things. You only despise them because of the curse. At one time they meant something to you." She picked up a golden doll and cocked her head.

Doing the wrong thing had hurt, so why did it hurt to try to do the right thing. I had to open up to her if I wanted her to open up to me. At the very least, she had a contract that could give my life back. "My daughter's. Before I touched her…"

Sorrow showed on her face. Not disgust or fear. Not sorrow for me being a greedy bastard. Sorry for the man who lost his daughter. She saw the good side of me, understood I'd made a mistake that millions of people made.

"You said your debts are from gambling?"

She nodded.

"Then paying them off once won't solve the problem." Tricky territory, but if she only loved me for my riches, and I gave them up, I wouldn't be able to keep her happy.

"I know." Her head hung low and I was desperate to push the hair out of her face, hold her, and do everything in my power to help her.

I eyed the paper on the table. Stepping past her, I touched one rock at a time, asking myself if I was a fool with each contact. It didn't matter. I'd rather be used than alone and feared.

She gasped. "You're doing it?"

Touching the last rock, I stood and grabbed the pen. Motioning to the rocks, I said, "They're all yours."

"Aren't you worried I'll still gamble?"

"Goldie, you took the biggest risk and helped me. In a few minutes, I may not have a Golden Touch anymore, but I'll do everything I can to help you work on your problems. And even if I can't help you, getting to hold you will be more than I ever thought I'd have."

She put her hands over her mouth as I opted to become a farmer and scrawled my name on the bottom of the page. No fanfare, no visit from Dionysus, no tingling of any kind.

Goldie inched her hand over the table and I instinctively pulled away.

Holding up a hand, I said, "Let's test it before I…"

My words trailed off at the thought of making a mistake. I walked outside and touched a rock. Nothing.

I picked the rock up to find a beetle underneath it, touched it, and nothing happened. Amazing. I controlled my breaths to stifle my elation.

Goldie stared with rapt attention.

Still fearful of touching her, being played by the gods, I walked back inside and touched her purse which she'd left on the counter. It remained her purse. My hands were clammy and I couldn't talk. I might truly be normal again. The promise of feeling her soft skin, kissing her perfect lips, and making love to her were a dream I never imagined could come true.

In a flash, Goldie rushed over, crashing into me and wrapping her arms around me tightly. For a moment I feared my curse wasn't fully lifted. Her muffled cries assured me she was very much alive. My heart was so full I swore it was going to burst, and my dick was in the same predicament.

I scooped her up, rushing her to the bedroom, letting her hands travel over my face, through my hair, down my neck, the supple feel of her body topping the list of the best things ever, but that was about to change. I sat her on the bed.

"I have to make love to you."

We both stripped our clothes and she laid back, watching as I crawled over her. I extended an arm to the drawer for a condom.

She shook her head.

I would have thought she was crazy, but I saw her rub my cum into herself earlier. With me coming inside of her, I'd shoot it a lot deeper. I put on the condom anyway. As much as I wanted to start a life with her, I wanted her to myself for a while.

After all, I was known to be greedy.

Seeing Red
By Rachel Kenley

Renata was the precious only daughter of a woodsman and his wife and lived a happy life in her small town. Her father's work was in great demand which often kept him busy and away from the house. When Renata's mother was mad at him, she claimed he loved the woods more than his family, but when the house was warm and there was a strong cooking fire, mother couldn't complain. As soon as her bothers were old enough they joined their father, and Renata and her mother were often alone to do what was necessary to tend to the house, the gardens and their small herd of animals. Renata learned all she needed from her mother and her grandmother who lived in a cottage in the woods. It was a quiet life in a quiet village.

As Renata grew older and grew more beautiful, her mother warned her about the boys who would soon be paying attention to her, but it was her Grandmother Willa who told her, on her 16th birthday, about the wolves. As gifts, her mother gave Renata a dagger to carry for protection. Her grandmother gave her a warm, heavy cloak lined completely inside with beautiful red satin. It was the most luxurious thing Renata ever owned and she knew she would cherish it

170

for all time, especially since her grandmother had one just like it.

"Why did you give her something with red," her mother complained. "It will attract all the wrong notice. A girl needs to be hidden and safe with dull colors like a bird so that predators won't be drawn to her."

"Nonsense," her grandmother said. "There are those we don't want to attract and those who need to know we are their friends."

"You are crazy, old woman," her mother said but Grandmother just smiled a knowing smile to Renata.

"Renata shall walk me back to my cottage tonight. I will send her home in the morning."

The walk to grandmother's house wasn't long when Renata was alone, but walking beside the older woman made the trip take longer. Still, Renata didn't mind. She was thrilled to have some time with her grandmother. Grandmother Willa always told the best stories and baked the most wonderful breads and sweets. She taught Renata what the woods could give them by pointing out what could be found in the forest that was good to eat or good for medicines. She treated Renata as a grown up, not as the baby in the family, and Renata worked hard to remember everything Willa taught and told her.

Once they got to Grandmother's cottage, Renata built up the fire from the embers in the fireplace, and it wasn't long before the room was warm and cozy. As her grandmother got ready for the night, Renata tidied up, moving things from higher shelves to lower locations now that her grandmother couldn't reach as easily.

Soon, Willa sat in her favorite chair, pulled a quilted blanket over her legs and said, "Come sit with me, my lovely granddaughter, for I have something I want to tell you."

Renata brought a chair from the table, took her grandmother's hand, and sat next to her. "Your mother thinks it's important to keep you hidden and safe until a proper suitor can be found for you, but it is time for you to know that you can have something much more special, much more magical than the men from your village."

"Magical?" Renata said.

"Magical," Willa repeated with a happy sigh, "and more wonderful and loving than you can ever imagine. In every other generation there is one daughter who is told of our legacy. As my grandmother told this to me on my 16th birthday, I now tell to you the connection between our family and the wolves."

"I know about the wolves, Grandmother. They come by night, hunt with stealth and steal the best of the animals. Sometimes they've been known to injure the men who get in their way and rarely are they killed and captured. They are to be feared especially on the nights of the full moon when they are at their strongest. Mother has told me to stay away from them."

"It is true that there are packs of wolves who come into villages to prey on whatever they can find. However, there are some wolves, my sweet child, who are so much more than that." And Grandmother Willa spun a tale of the wolves who changed.

Renata could hardly sleep for the stories her

grandmother told her and of the heritage she could claim when she was older. The one thing she knew for certain, however, was that when the time came she was going to do as her grandmother told her. Burrowing under her beautiful new cloak and thinking of what it might bring her when she wore the red side out, she finally fell asleep.

Over the next several years, Renata's life continued as it had been. As she neared 18, the boys of the town paid her more and more attention although she did nothing to encourage their advances—and frequently used her dagger to discourage them. Her mother hoped Renata would choose a man to marry, but Renata turned down even the best hunters who would have made fine spouses. Her mother tried to convince her husband to have a match arranged but with a look to Renata that she understood, he never agreed.

Then the worst winter anyone could remember came and Renata lost her father and her beloved grandmother within a few months. Just that past spring her oldest brother met and married a woman from a nearby village and moved out of the house to start a family of his own. With the passing of her father, her second brother became the man of the house and not long after he too married. Fortunately, Grandmother Willa had left her cottage to her granddaughter and soon after his wife joined them, Renata decided it was time to leave her family.

Her mother claimed a woman couldn't live in the woods by herself. It was dangerous and inappropriate. Again she tried to convince her daughter to choose one of the village men, but Renata would not be swayed.

She promised that if she had not chosen a husband within one year's time, she would come home and her mother could choose for her. Still concerned, but believing Renata would ultimately not like living so isolated and would return, her mother agreed.

Her brother and his wife helped Renata on the day she moved out, carrying her possessions, basic food stuffs to help her get started, as well as two chickens, two goats and two pigs so she would have all she needed. He, too, was concerned about Renata's decision, but since his wife had told him the night before that she was carrying a child, he decided perhaps this was for the best.

When they arrived, her brother was again uneasy about leaving her. He had never seen their grandmother's cottage and was troubled about her living in such a small space. "Are you certain there is enough here for you?"

"I have a three rooms all to myself, brother. I shall be fine." Then Renata showed her brother the different stores of herbs and other dried goods her grandmother had kept at the cottage. In the months since Willa died, Renata visited the cottage often to make certain everything was intact and in good shape. He offered her a weekly allowance to help her purchase what she needed in town which she accepted gratefully. As much as she was looking forward to being on her own, there was love in her family, and she knew how lucky she was.

Renata breathed a sigh of relief when she was finally alone. She walked around her home, which felt new to her now that she knew she would not be leaving. She ran her hands over familiar items and was happier than she could remember being since her grandmother's passing. She quickly got to work baking bread and making herself dinner, and soon the house filled with the scents of good cooking. Later that night, she took her place in Willa's chair before the fire. As she opened a book to read she thought she heard the cry of a wolf in the distance.

For the next few weeks, Renata created a routine for herself. She'd wake early, take care of the animals, and bake what she needed for herself and to sell in the village for extra money. Most of her afternoons were spent walking in the woods wearing her beautiful cape as she searched for herbs for medicine as well as berries, mushrooms and other edibles.

And always she listened for the wolves.

She couldn't say how she knew, but she was aware that the wolves had noticed her since she moved into the woods. And there was one in particular who occasionally came closer than the others. She saw him a few times from a distance, beautiful night black fur with the bluest of eyes, but if she tried to approach or look for him, he would disappear.

After a few months, Renata decided it was time to act on her legacy. She set out extra rabbit and squirrel traps before going to the village to get what she needed for the next several days. She didn't intend to leave her cottage until the waning of the full moon.

Trips into the village were often troublesome. Even though on these visits she never wore the cloak her grandmother gave her, she attracted attention from several of the young men who were looking to marry. One in particular was quite insistent on getting her notice. Joseph was considered by many to be the best hunter in the area, and her mother, when Renata saw her, encouraged her to make the match.

"He can provide for you. You will be well taken care of." Renata tried to explain her disinterest—as well as her ability to hunt for herself as necessary—but still her mother pushed and cajoled. Renata would not be swayed. Besides the legacy she intended to pursue, there was something about him that made her uncomfortable. She knew he couldn't be trusted.

Today was no different. As Renata walked away from the shepherd's home having bought several new bundles of fleece she found Joseph waiting for her by the gate.

"Where are you off to, my pretty one?"

"As this was my last stop, I am heading home."

"Then I shall accompany you to make sure that you are safe."

"Thank you for the offer, Joseph, but that is not necessary."

"A woman should not be alone in the woods. It's dangerous."

"I know how to keep myself safe from all kinds of predators," she said. "As you well know." She looked to his forearm where she'd once cut him with her dagger when he'd gotten too close.

He grunted but still fell into step beside her. As they walked through the village she knew others were looking at them, making assumptions. She bore it knowing this would be the last time she'd have to worry about him.

When they got to the edge of the woods she stopped. "Good day, Joseph," she said, hoping he would finally leave her. She never had guests who weren't family at the cottage, and she certainly was not going to invite him.

"I would see you to your door."

"And I would see myself."

"What kind of a gentleman would I be if I didn't take you all the way home?"

"The kind that listens to what a woman requests," she said. He took her arm and started to say something but a growl from the woods had him stepping back and away. Renata couldn't help but smile as she walked confidently into the shadow of the woods leaving Joseph behind. *Thank you,* she whispered and thought she heard a chuff in response.

She got to her home, left her packages on the center table, then went back into the woods to collect the trapped animals. She brought them, still alive, into the stone room at the back of the house. Most of the time the room was used for storage and drying, but her grandmother explained it was built with an additional purpose in mind.

The sun was setting and Renata hurried to make the room ready. In addition to the animals, she placed fresh hay on the floor and water in a large pail. She made her dinner and tried to eat slowly, but her excitement was too much. She'd been waiting for this day for years.

Tonight would be the night. She was sure of it.

As the moon reached its zenith she walked into the woods making certain to wear her beautiful cape, this time with the red side facing out. She hadn't walked long before she heard something behind her. To be certain, she continued deeper into the woods and once she was confident she was being followed, she turned and started a slow walk back to her cottage, listening all the while. As soon as she saw the cottage in the distance, she picked up her pace. Whoever was following her gave chase, just as she'd hoped.

Her heart racing with both hope and anxiety, she dashed into the stone room, the door of which was left open, the wolf nearly at her heels. Once inside, she ran into the house, slammed the door behind her, then pulled the lever that would drop the heavy wooden door and close off any escape from the stone room. A loud howl followed the banging of the door.

She had done it. She had trapped a wolf.

And if her grandmother's stories were true, not just any wolf, but a wolf who was actually a man with the ability to change at will between forms except during the full moon.

Renata leaned against door that separated the stone room from the rest of the cottage. She could hear the wolf banging himself on the walls. Her grandmother had warned her this would be the most dangerous time. He would be at full strength and would do anything to free himself. As hard as it was, she needed to wait until he calmed down. She pulled her chair by the door, sat with her knitting and quietly sang to him until she fell asleep.

The next morning all was quiet in the house and in the stone room. Renata prepared herself breakfast and after she'd eaten she lifted the thin-hinged flap that was at the bottom of the door that connected the stone room to the rest of the house. This, her grandmother explained, allowed her to slide him food as it was necessary and to enable him to get used to her sound and scent.

"I'm here, black wolf," she said and tried to sound calm. She'd been told that there were some wolves who could not be tamed and the women who caught them paid the ultimate price. Since this wolf had been near her before, she hoped this meant he had an interest in her and not an interest in killing her. "I know you do not like being caged." There was a bang on the door as if to emphasis his agreement. "I am part of a long legacy, generations of women who have done this. My grandmother and hers before were wolf women, and I am one too. It is my destiny to claim you as my mate."

There was silence from the other side. She did not know what that meant but since he was no longer trying to break through the door, she took it as a good sign. "If you haven't noticed there is food for you as well as water. I will catch you more fresh meat and give you water when you need it, but I will not open this door until you are able to shift back into your human form."

This time there was a snort. He may not be able to communicate with words, but it was clear he understood what she was saying.

For the next day Renata went about her normal routine but kept up a one-sided conversation with the wolf who remained her captive. She was heartened each time she heard the wolf made a sound in response to something she said. It was exactly as her Grandmother had told her.

"If he's right for you, you'll know and so will he. I saw your grandfather, in his wolf form, for months before I was able to capture him. After holding him for three nights, there was no doubt in my mind that he was the man—and wolf—I was meant to be with."

"How could you know? He was a wolf."

"Oh, he was so much more than that, my sweet. If you choose to embrace our family's legacy, you'll discover this for yourself."

Something occurred to Renata. "So my father..."

"Is part wolf, yes. It's one of the reasons he chose a profession that requires him to be away from his family for periods of time. This clan of wolves can change or not change at will, except for the three nights of the full moon. Until it a few hours before dawn on the third night, they must remain a wolf. He protected all of you from this knowledge by being away on nights of the change."

"And my brothers?"

"I don't believe they can change. You will need to keep our secret if you choose to accept to be a part of this line of women."

Renata had wanted this from the moment she heard the stories, but hadn't known when she would go through with the process until the first time she saw the beautiful black wolf a few months before her 18th birthday. She was drawn to him and believed— hoped—he was drawn to her, that he was the one who'd frightened Joseph the day before.

And now he was hers.

Well, perhaps. Only time would tell if after his captivity ended he would stay, but with each response he offered she was more hopeful. When he needed something he gave a short howl and on the second day when she'd gone out and stayed longer than she said she would, he gave her a sharp bark on her return. She smiled as she apologized. She liked the idea that he was protective, that he worried. She could hardly wait for dawn the on the third day when she would be able to meet him as a man.

On that final day she did everything later and slower, trying to make the time go faster. It didn't work. It was nearly 8:00 when she finished her dinner, and she didn't know what to do to keep herself busy. She'd tried spinning earlier but her threads were uneven and she gave up rather than ruin the whole bundle. Her mending was sloppy, her knitting needed to be pulled out.

"Maybe I should go out for a walk and pick some of the night blooming herbs. I'm low on a few I will need in the coming months. That would keep me busy." An angry bark came in reply. "I won't be very long. They aren't far from the cottage and, as you know, I have the light of the moon to guide me."

The bark came again, doubled.

"But, I…" The bark that interrupted her was so loud she jumped and put her hand to her heart. This was more than a simple no. "Very well. I suppose I could read. Shall I read aloud for us again?" She'd done this the night before and enjoyed having him listen. Some thought it was silly for a woman to read, but her grandmother had insisted and the world of stories kept her companies on many nights. She waited for his response and when a black paw came out from under the door opening, she reached out and stroked his beautiful fur. "Reading it is. But if I run out of cereus this month, it is your fault."

That earned her a chuff that sounded distinctly like laughter.

She made herself some chamomile tea, got comfortable in her chair and began to read where she'd left off. When she'd fallen asleep she couldn't say but she was woken sometime later by a knock at the door. Foggy with sleep she went to open it but a hushed bark made her stop. Right, it was foolish to open the door to an unknown visitor.

"Who is it?"

"It's Joseph, Renata. I was out hunting and I tripped and hurt my leg. May I come in?"

"Why are you out so late?"

"So that the game can't see me. In the quiet I hunt better."

"It's not so far back to the village. Can't you make it there?"

"No, I don't think so. Please, Renata, I'm hurt. I need to rest and to have you go to the village for me in the morning. Don't turn me away."

The wolf gave a low growl that rumbled through Renata, but she assumed it was because another man was intruding on their time. She didn't want to let Joseph in and worried if he would discover the captive wolf, but she couldn't have him stay outside when he was hurt and she could help. She unlatched the door and opened it.

It took less than a breath to know she'd made a mistake. Joseph pushed his way in when the door was only an inch or two open. As he stumbled past her she knew he wasn't injured—he was drunk. She could smell it on him. And she knew from the few times her father and brothers had come home in this state that he could be very dangerous.

"Have a seat by the fire, Joseph," she said in a calm voice and hoped he didn't hear the wolf as clearly as she did. "Let me see what I can get for your leg."

She pulled some tinctures down from the shelves and grabbed a bottle of belladonna. Her grandmother had used it for pain in her joints as she got older and Renata knew that a large enough dose would knock Joseph out for hours.

"What I want from you has nothing to do with my leg," he said grabbing her from behind. Renata screamed and fought him as dragged her toward the bedroom. "You've made me the laughing stock of the village. 'Joseph can bring down a stag but not a wee rabbit who lives in the woods.' Well I'll show them and you. Tonight you'll be mine and tomorrow I'll bring you before the preacher to make it legal."

As he pulled, Renata did everything she could to get out of his grip. She kicked and scratched and finally bent her face to his hand and bit his wrist. That got him to release her and she ran for the door that held the wolf but she was only able to move the latch a little before he was on her again. "Let me go," she screamed and fought. "Or I'll tell everyone you forced me."

"Who would believe you? You let me in. I didn't need to break the door down. Poor trusting Renata. You've been on your own for too long. It's clear you need a man to keep you safe."

"Help," she cried.

"Who can hear you, silly woman? There's no one near. You're mine and no one is going to stop me."

She tried to scramble for the stone room again, but Joseph bent low to push himself at her abdomen and as she bent over from the force, he threw her over his shoulder. Renata heard the angry calls of the wolf, saw the door shudder with each slam of the wolf's body against the wood, but despaired of help coming from him.

In three long strides they were in her bedroom. Joseph tossed her onto the mattress and put his knee on her chest as he undid the fastenings on his pants. "Don't fight and it will go easier on you."

She looked around for something to use as a weapon but before she could there was a thunderous crack as wood splintered in the other room. The roar that ensued was almost deafening, and it was followed by the appearance of a huge black wolf in the doorway.

"What in the name of..." but that was all Joseph said before the wolf was upon him, pushing him off Renata and onto the floor. The man tried to fight but it was no use. The wolf was stronger, mad with rage, and focused on his prey. One bite to the throat and Joseph lay still in a puddle of his own blood.

Renata and the wolf stayed as they were a moment, staring at the body, both unsure of what to say or do. Renata got her thoughts together first. She threw herself at the wolf, wrapping her arms around his neck and burying her face against his fur. "Thank you, thank you," she said not holding back the tears of relief that poured from her.

She didn't know how long she held him before she felt strong arms come around her. Human arms. "You're welcome," said a deep voice. She straightened her head to see if she was imagining things, but the man who had been a wolf pulled away. "Don't look. I am bloody from the kill. Let me clean up before you see me."

"Of course," she said and stepping back she went

quickly to the other room for water and a cloth. She brought him both, then went into the main room to wait.

It wasn't long before he came into the room with the blanket from her bed wrapped around his waist. She gasped to look upon her wolf for the first time in this form.

He was magnificent. Tall and muscular with dark hair on his head, chest and arms. His shoulders were broad and his face was in need of a shave. And his eyes were bluer than a clear summer sky. "What big eyes you have," she said, unsure of what else to say.

"All the better for seeing you with. Are you alright?" he asked.

She wanted to run to him, to feel his arms around her again, but found herself suddenly shy in the presence of this a powerful man, one she had kept prisoner for almost three days. "I am," she managed.

"We have things to discuss, but first I must ask if you have some simple cloth that I can use to clean the mess in the other room. After that, I will bring him into the woods and leave him to be discovered. It will be assumed he was killed by a wild animal, which he was." The last part was said with a smile.

She brought him what he requested and as he did what was necessary with the remains of Joseph, she picked up the pieces of door he shattered when he came to save her. When he returned he was wearing pants and a shirt, which surprised her.

As if reading her confusion he said, "These are my woods. I am here often, as you know. I left these when I transformed on the first night of the full moon. Before you lured me to your home."

"I know that might have been wrong of me…" She stopped when he crossed to her and placed a finger on her lips.

"You are a descendant of Willa. Daughter of a kinsman of mine. I know what you did, and why, Renata."

"You know my name?"

"I have been watching you for quite some time, but you know that as well," he said. She loved the sound of his voice. Deep and smooth with a hint at the danger and strength that lay beneath the surface.

"I didn't know. I hoped."

"Now you know."

"I don't know your name."

"I am Valko, and I am yours."

Her heart gave a lurch. Part of her worried that even after he came to her rescue, and the time they'd spent together, he might not wish to stay. Her grandmother told her wolves cannot be forced to mate, but once they did, it was forever. "I've wanted that so very much."

"As I watched you, I thought of approaching, but was unsure of what you knew or if you could be trusted with my secret. Then I saw your red cape which told me all I needed."

"You're not mad about being trapped in the room."

"Well, it wasn't my favorite way to spend the full moon, but I know the stories of the woman who are destined to mate with my kind. This form of pursuit and capture happens in every tribe, in every generation. Apparently, it was my time."

"What happens next?"

"I am going to make you mine."

For the second time that night a man pulled Renata into his arms but this time she wasn't afraid, this time she didn't need to fight.

This time she surrendered.

It didn't take long before they were in her bedroom and he'd rid them both of their clothes. She'd never been naked with a man before and for a moment she felt unsure, but then he kissed her, stroked her hair and caressed her back and breasts. As she melted under his touch and came alive for him, her confidence and desire grew.

His kiss was warm and powerful. She never imagined how wonderful it could feel to be naked in the arms of a man she desired. She knew of intercourse from her mother and grandmother, but words had nothing on the experience. They continued kissing until he moved his mouth away to kiss and touch all she had exposed to him. He leaned her back against the pillow and moved to lick her nipples, blowing on the damp peaks to make them harder. She shivered at the cold, enjoying the new feeling. His mouth was soft, his beard rough and the combination of sensations added to her pleasure.

He worked his way down, exploring every inch of her body and she gasped when his fingers first touched her pussy and the electricity that passed through her had her calling out his name. He put his hands between her thighs and pulled, gently showing her he wanted her to open her legs. As soon as she did, his fingers were there, caressing her opening. A rush of heat pooled where he touched and she couldn't stop the sigh.

"You're wet. Do you know what that means?"

"Yes, it means my body is prepared for sexual intercourse."

"It means more than that. Some women can be touched and not get wet at all. You are showing me you can accept and enjoy pleasure, welcome it. Especially from me. You want me."

"I do," she whispered, feeling the truth in every part of her body. "I do want you."

He bent forward and for the first time she experienced the touch of a man's mouth on her pussy. Nothing could have allowed her to imagine the flare of desire that enflamed her. The intimacy of being spread for him with his tongue laving her most sensitive skin coupled with the feelings of joy made her want to scream if only release some of the intensity. She moaned and gripped the sheets with all of her might. If the pleasure increased, she might shred them completely.

It increased.

Valko's tongue explored her most secret folds and where his mouth didn't touch, his fingers did. The combination was almost too much. She raked her fingers through his hair, down his shoulders, touching him wherever she could reach, wanting him more with every passing moment. And then there was a shift deep inside her belly.

"Something is happening," she told him as the sensations amplified. "I can't. I'm not sure…"

"Let go, my love."

And she did. Pleasure built in her and what had been a slow climb now became a raging torrent, rushing toward a crest unlike any she had ever imagined. Her climax hit her with the force of a tornado. Need, desire, passion and release all swirled together in a vortex that had her sitting up, crying out his name, and gushing onto his tongue.

She'd teased out orgasms with her own fingers in the quiet of her bedroom, but none compared to the intensity of the one created by someone she loved. This was beyond imagining, beyond words.

"My sweet, responsive, Renata."

Renata could hear her heartbeat ringing in her ears. Her body was overheated and more sensitive than she thought possible. Still sitting up, resting on her elbows, she watched as he continued to lick and stroke her, more softly now, teasing out shudders and shivers.

Sated as she was, she knew there was something more. Some other need calling to her, and as she turned to look at his body she knew what that was. She brought him to her, felt the heat and weight of him against her body, top to bottom. She caressed his shoulders and back, marveling at his size, and as she learned the places that made him sigh, she reached between them and wrapped her fingers around his hard cock.

That earned her a growl.

"The wolf is never far away, is he?"

"Not when you are near me like this," he said. "Are you ready? Will you join with me?"

"Yes," she whispered, her voice unfamiliar to her ears.

He positioned himself and entered her slowly. "A moment's pain and I will do all I can to bring you pleasure again."

She nodded, trusting him. The tip of his cock entered her and she took a breath, doing what she could to stay relaxed as he stretched her, filled her. He kissed her deeply and as she melted into the passion of his embrace there was a quick sensation of tearing, sharp stinging and followed a burn which melted into something more.

He lifted his head to look into her eyes and she fell into the pool of blue. They were one.

Valko pulled back, filled her again, then repeated the movement. It wasn't long before she matched his thrusts, met his need with her own. His moans matched hers and as her pleasure increased she knew his did as well. She wrapped her legs around him, let him lift her off the bed with his strength, let him set the pace so that they would both be pleased.

As his cries intensified she knew his peak was near and she reveled in being able to give him pleasure as he had given her. When he spilled himself inside of her she cried with the joy overflowing in her heart.

"Did I hurt you, my love?" he asked seeing her tears.

"There was the moment you said and then nothing but bliss. I have heard some of the village girls speak with near horror of their first times. This was nothing like that. Of course, you are nothing like the men they are tied to."

"This is quite true," he said and kissed her again.

As she lay on his chest listening to his heart beat, he said, "I heard stories growing up of the women who were destined to love a wolf. I thought they were silly tales made up by the elders to make sure we kept a careful eye on humans. Then I saw you as you left your grandmother's home, this home, one day. I watched you walk through the woods as though you had nothing to fear. Then you turned and saw me and in that moment I knew you were my mate, knew that I would find a way to be with you."

"And so you have."

"We found each other. And now, my heart, if you're not tired, I find I still hunger for you."

"What will you do about it?"

"Why, I'm going to eat you up."

Grendel's Love
By Alice Kay

In days long gone, a lonely widow woman was exiled by fate to live in the marshlands with her boy-child, Grendel. The widow and her boy were of noble birth and once lived in a castle with their kin by their side, until such time as thieving tribes of Scyldings crossed the water. Crippling conflicts raged across their land as feudal warriors fought vicious battles to take or to hold the blood-dwellings of the once great kings lost to the ages.

On the day the boy turned 10, the castle of his ancestors was taken by fire and sword. From a window of a watchtower, the boy whimpered on spying his father, a brave and godly knight, wounded and dying in the dirt beneath the mighty battle shield of his liege-lord. Even as women screamed and towers burned, Grendel ran to his father to say good-bye. The boy's shirt caught fire as he ran and, with his clothes aflame, he reached his father as the man took his last breath.

A battle-weary warrior took pity on the boy and tossed him in the mud of a pig sty to douse the flames. Grendel lay covered in muck as the battle wound down. His distraught mother found him near invisible in the mud and close to death. Gathering up the wounded boy, she fled the chaotic scene, carrying the mute, scarred, fatherless, friendless boy and escaping with his charred body deep into the forest.

Grendel, the dead knight's offspring and the widow's son, with fire-scarred skin and a limp to his walk, survived the horror. He lived and grew to superior size and strength, a giant of a man with a bone-crushing grip. Unable to say a last good-bye to his beloved father, he never regained his speech. On lonely, moonstruck nights, he sent out blood-curling howls in memory of all he lost.

In a cold, damp cavern found under a pool and close to the sea, the widow and son made a home. The destitute mother spent her time lamenting their fate and singing her sorrow to the winds. Grendel spent his boyhood years as a shadow stealing food and spying on the Scyldings scattered around what was once his homeland. As he aged alone with only his fragmented mother lost in a world of her own, he haunted the moors with a hard-heart and a gruesome visage, seeking revenge.

On many dark nights as the moon slipped behind clouds and the castle lights dimmed, the once noble boy slipped into the halls of his enemies, adeptly entering the chambers of the sleeping men as though he were a great, hulking nightmare and not a simple boy. When the kitchens were quiet and the wine cellars shuttered, the dirt-smeared, hungry boy found ways to take the best of their meats and cheeses, along with their finest wines, despite the heavily armed guards in and around the castle.

The moors were his first love, the vast empty space driving him to explore and triumph in minor skirmishes with the wild creatures which he ate as their warm blood ran down his face. Travelers feared crossing the moors as rumors spread of a monster living on the plain. If the traveler were a Scylding, he had reason to fear. As the boy grew into a young man, he sought his revenge on the enemies of his people. Though not reduced to cannibalism, he had no problem with killing the men of his wrath, flinging apart their bodies and setting the stage so men believed he ate their flesh as he had seen done on the battlefields of his enemy.

The Scyldings ruled their stolen lands with an iron fist, cowering the locals into submission, except for the mysterious monster of the moors. The creature remained hidden from sight despite the troops engaged to track it down and capture or kill the great beast which haunted their dreams. Though the fighting had ended, and peace spread across the land, Grendel spied on the Scyldings with growing anger as they abused his once great tribe with their demands.

One day, near the same riverbank where Grendel had played with his cousins in the long ago, outside the castle of the pilfering King, Grendel spied from the shadows a glorious young woman with a familiar face from his childhood. Muddled memories broke loose of unsullied times before the fighting began. *Judith*. He remembered a time when he chased the red-headed Judith along this riverbank, scattering a swarm of butterflies. A sharp pain to his heart drew him back from the memory, as though it were fire.

Grendel settled back on the ground, hidden by reeds and grass, a hand clutched to a cleaving tightness inside his chest. *Judith*. Time flowed and the tightness of his heart loosened as he watched Judith undress and bathe in the flowing waters. Her form was unlike any he had seen before. Certainly not like the skinny bones and sagging skin of his mother.

Judith was lush and healthy as a young roe running wild on the plains. Her breasts enchanted him, the flow of her hips drove him mad. He nearly called out to his old friend, but a rustling in the grass stopped him. A man in the colors of a Scylding guard spied on Judith as she bathed. The hot blood of anger whipped through Grendel's veins. The man had no right to spy on Judith. He had no right to spy on anyone from Judith's tribe.

With little thought to stealth and cunning, Grendel rushed the man, knocking him to the ground and wrestling him to his back. The Scylding faced him with a look of horror as Grendel wrapped his arm around his neck to give a sharp twist.

A sound of alarm caused Grendel to look up. Judith stood above him with her clothing held in one hand to cover her body, her other hand covering her mouth in shock by the violence. Her wide eyes examined the dead man's face.

"I know him," she said. "He's been following me, hoping to find me alone I'm sure." She raised her eyes to meet Grendel's and he saw her shudder at the sight of him. He knew he looked bad and smelled even worse. Grendel shifted his face to one side to hide the scarring, but there was nothing he could do about the dirt and grime. He seldom bathed, using the mud and grass as camouflage as he hunted in the wilds or stalked through the castle in the dark of night.

Instead of running like she should, Judith continued to stare at him. "Who are you?" she asked.

Grendel shrugged. He was nobody. And he had stopped speaking so long ago, he was unsure he could say his name even if he tried.

"It's alright," Judith said. "You need to go. If they find you here…"

Taking her advice, he climbed off the limp body of the Scylding guard, backing away low in the grass. Before he left, he looked again in Judith's eyes and thought he saw alarm, fear…and pity. The last caused another bout of anger. No one had reason to pity Grendel. He rose and strode away, hardening his heart against the woman. No one.

Grendel ran for hours across the empty moors toward the sea. At times, he swiped at his mud-laden face, angry at Judith for not recognizing her old friend and angry at himself and his mother for hiding themselves away. He could have survived under the Scylding rulers, maybe even fought back.

Grendel last returned home to his mother and his cave two moons ago, sleeping in the wilds for too long. He slowed to take in signs of prey in the area. Mother would want meat when he returned. He found stones to throw. When he threw hard, the stones could drop a roe if he spotted one. If not, she'd be satisfied with a grouse. After so long living off fish and rodents, she'd be pleased with anything he brought.

When Grendel made his way back to the cavern, he carried two partridges with him. In her delight to see him, his mother would not stop touching him with her thin skeleton hands even though he tried to brush her away. He took a closer look at her in the firelight and saw the truth of how she was. Another tooth had fallen out and her scalp showed through her thinning hair. As he sat before the fire and listened to her ceaseless, nonsensical chatter, he tried to see her as she was before but his early memories were blocked by fire.

Moved by how wild his mother looked, and how Judith looked at him, he dove into the deep cold pool inside the cave, loosening the dried mud and wiping it away. He cleaned and scrubbed until there was no piece of him which was not clean. His mother watched, drooping over her walking stick with her mouth hanging open.

"Grendel, what's wrong with you?" she cried.

* * *

Judith woke from a deep sleep. She'd been dreaming of the murder but her dream wasn't a nightmare as it should have been. The dream comforted her, even though details floated away. She tried to catch them but all she remembered was his eyes. So familiar, and so safe, even as he twisted the Scylding's neck. She wanted to return to the dream. Wanted to stay there longer. Instead, she forced herself awake and into her nightmare world.

The sun was coming up and she had chores to do. King Holofernes returned from the far lands today and a great feast was planned. She had to help her aunt and the others with the preparations in the kitchen. Putting on her worn woolen dress, she belted it firmly on her thin waist. If she hurried, there might be a clean linen apron to put over it in the kitchen.

When she arrived at the large fire pit in the Meade hall where the Scyldings would gather for their feast, she stopped to stare into the flames and recognition dawned as she saw reflected there the eyes of Grendel. Both the boy Grendel had been and the man he had become. Grendel, the boy on fire. Grendel, the monster of the moors. He was the killer amongst them. He was the legend haunting the land. Her heart palpitated, not with fear but with hope.

Judith went about her chores as if in a fog, her thoughts returning again and again to the time before. To the time she had seen Grendel catch on fire. And now to the time that he lived. By the end of the day, she knew she had to find him. To tell him she knew his secret. But her heart carried fear. The man was wild. She'd seen it for herself. He was a monster to those living here. And bigger than life to those who had to cross the moors. Grendel put fear into the hearts of enemies and friends alike. There would be no forgiveness. The man was a monster. Although...he had never harmed anyone from her tribe. The deaths had all been Scyldings. Was he a monster or was he not? She had to find out for herself.

Before the next day dawned, Judith packed a bag and kissed her auntie goodbye. Her parents had died in the same battle which had taken Grendel's father. The tribe had burned the bodies for days, and the stench of it could never be forgotten. Everyone in the tribe worked hard to pacify their new lords, those who rebelled were put to death. Each day since the invasion had been a struggle to survive. A tear fell from her eye. She was a woman now and would be forced to bear a Scylding child. She would find Grendel and beg for his help. And if he refused, she would throw herself into the sea.

After two hours of walking, Judith flung her pack on the ground and dropped down beside it. The land was flat and empty for as far as she could see. Finding Grendel on the moors would be impossible. Strong, hardy men had been searching for years. A hawk noticed her from far away and flew closer for a better look.

That was it! If she found a high point, Grendel could find her. He'd come in for a closer look, and they would find each other. Judith's heart jumped with the joy of her plan, never considering what might happen to her once he did find her. Whatever happened to Grendel in his life, whatever else he had done, Grendel had saved her from that evil man.

Her heart soared, only to sink again. Why had Grendel not spoken to her? What secrets did he hide as he roamed the barren moors?

* * *

Two days after returning to his mother, Grendel had gone out again. Her endless, meaningless words had been too much to bear. She'd pleaded with him not to leave her alone again. The confinement of the cavern squeezed him until it became difficult to breath. He might as well be on a Scylding torture rack as remain in the cave, away from the freedom of the moors and the starlit skies.

He promised to return soon and set out. As the sky darkened, a flame on the edge of a cliff caught his eye. The fire was about an hour's run from where he hunted game, and it looked to be man-made. Scyldings? He ran his hands on his trousers. What would they be doing so far out? Hunting him again because of that man? His thoughts turned to Judith and the way the water had slid off her back when she rose from her bath in the river.

He tried to smile at the memory, but it felt awkward and unfamiliar on his face. The woman had been frightened of him. Worse, she had pitied him. He needed to wipe the memory of her from his mind before it destroyed what little he had left. His dreams were filled with the sound of battle in a world he could not escape. Horrid screaming and the sight of blood. He held tight to those dreams. They fueled his revenge.

Picking up his axe and a handful of stones to refill the pouch on his side, he headed toward the cliff wanting nothing more than to find the bloodlust which allowed him to kill.

With his usual stealth, he made his way to the fire, alert to every sound in the dark night. As he approached the campfire, he saw one lone figure asleep on the ground. He strode quietly to the sleeping man, axe at the ready, only to discover the delicate features and red hair of Judith curled up in the blanket.

Startled by the surprise, he let out a grunt and she woke. They both froze in place, Grendel standing over the young woman with an axe in his hand, breathing deep with unfamiliar emotions flowing through his veins.

Judith spoke first, "Grendel?" she asked in a gentle, shy voice.

When he nodded, she rose to her feet keeping the blanket wrapped around her for warmth. "I knew it!" she said and reached out to him.

Grendel stepped back, fearful, untrusting, alone for so long with only his batty mother for company, he had to think back to what Judith wanted from him. His mind slipped beyond the veil of the fire to a simple memory of when he was young. To a time of running to his mother for comfort, for a hug.

Judith watched him with intensity, as if she understood his discomfort with people. Not for long though. Once the memory kicked in, he dropped his axe, spread his arms, and Judith stepped into his arms as if they'd never been parted by war.

After the hug, Judith took a few steps back, suddenly shy. This was not the same man she'd seen commit murder on the side of the river. That man had been wild and untamed, covered in filth, and hostile as a fire-breathing dragon. This Grendel was cleaned up and had a surprisingly handsome face, despite the burn marks on one side. The scarring began below his left ear, running along his jaw and under his chin where it broadened as it made its way to his chest. She wanted to see under his shirt. How much of his body had burnt that night?

Judith learned soon enough that Grendel couldn't, or wouldn't, speak and decided the easiest way to communicate was by asking yes and no questions. As the moon cycled through the sky and they spent the days and nights renewing their childhood friendship, they developed their own personal sign language. Others did the hunting and foraging for her tribe and Judith had spent little time in the wilderness. She did know how to put together a good meal over the fire and was pleased to see Grendel enjoy her cooking.

* * *

During their time together on the moors, Grendel taught her how to survive off the land, and he even introduced Judith to his mother. As far as Judith could tell, the woman was a lunatic who made no sense with the things she said. Judith nodded her head politely and allowed the woman to paw at her with her bony hands. Grendel's mother frightened her, but the cavern itself was a find. She wanted to explore the gold and treasure piled along the back wall.

"Grendel, did you steal this?" she asked.

He hung his head in embarrassment, then gave her a shy look and nodded. She placed a hand on his cheek. "You did a good job. When we rid the Scyldings from our land, we can sell the treasure for all of our tribe."

Grendel grinned, and it no longer felt so odd on his face. He placed his hand over hers, drew it to his lips, and kissed it. His heart filled with an emotion he'd never experienced before.

* * *

Judith was glad when they returned to the open space of the moors. Although she enjoyed the sound of the sea from the cavern, the space was too confining with Grendel's mother muttering and hovering around her all the time. Most of what she said was vile and repugnant. She could tell Grendel loved the old woman though and tried his best to care for her. And, she thought, his mother had been the one to save Grendel's life. For that, Judith was grateful. She gazed at Grendel with admiration. He had survived so much and yet his heart was nothing but kind and gentle.

It was a pitch-dark night and they were sleeping on the beach when they heard the Scyldings come. The neigh of a horse jolted Judith awake. Fear stoked her blood and panic ensued. She looked around the campsite for Grendel before remembering he had taken meat to his mother. She loved this little cove, and she'd insisted on staying here alone until he returned the next day.

The horses galloped along the beach, their hooves landing with muffled thuds. She couldn't begin to count them. She had to hide. Running to the brushes, she was nearly there when one of the animals broke off from the herd and galloped towards her. She tried to dive into the bushes, but a hand reached out and grabbed the back of her dress to lift her. She could only see the black of his boots as she faced the sand, but that was enough to tell her he was a Scylding warrior.

Judith kicked the air and tried to beat on his arm and wiggle free, but all she could do was flail.

"Stop it, girl. You're going with us." The warrior placed her on the horse in front of him and kept a tight arm around her waist. "I know someone who wants to speak with you." The warrior barked an order. "Get her things."

There were no more words spoken as the troop of Scyldings turned their horses and rode back to their stolen castle as fast as the animals could go. They arrived mid-day and she was locked in a room near the kitchens.

"Rest up, girl. They need help with the feast tonight."

* * *

Grendel returned to the campsite the next day to find Judith gone and the campsite empty. His heart sank. He thought she liked him, that she might even stay with him, but she had returned to the tribe instead. He couldn't blame the kind, young woman. A lady had no business living an isolated life on the moors. Look what it had done to his mother.

He kicked at a blackened log on the dead campfire. His insides matched the cold, black wood and he watched as the log rolled toward the bushes. The sun struck a piece of metal lying in the sand between the log and the vegetation. Grendel strode over to pick it up, recognizing it immediately. The golden bird-of-prey. The Scyldings wore them on their armpieces.

Hot blood rushed through Grendel's veins. They had taken her. The Scyldings had taken his Judith. Grendel raised his head and howled out his anger. The bushes shook as nearby, all the birds and creatures fled from the scene.

Grendel ran for hours, headed straight for the castle, and it was late in the evening when he arrived. He rested at the edge of the river where he had first seen Judith, and then put on the armor of mud and grass as he'd often worn to sneak through the shadows. With anger and sadness and great stealth, the man-monster glided through an empty passage and watched through a peephole at the night's beastly feasting of drunken men. Judith walked among them, a tray of mugs on her hip and a hard expression on her face. She spilled a container of meade on one of the Scylding warriors, on purpose, Grendel was sure of it. The warrior jumped up, his arm pulled back to strike her and Grendel seethed. Another man put a stop to the strike or Grendel would have rampaged through the crowd.

The wicked ones continued to drink, and the fortress grew thick with night air. There had to be at least thirty men in the room. Grendel's fists opened and closed in fury, but he had to bide his time. After the meal, a guard grabbed Judith around the waist, hauling her to the stairs. Another guard followed behind, laughing as she squirmed to get away. A red heat possessed Grendel as he listened to the unfamiliar words of the filthy men, understanding enough to learn Judith was to be a slave-gift to Holofernes, leader of Grendel's enemies and tyrant of Judith's tribe. The loathsome Scyldings needed no words as their laughter and actions spoke loudly of the pending rape and defilement of the girl.

* * *

Judith, her clothing stripped away by the guards, waited alone in the sinister chambers of Holofernes. She knew nothing of her champion in the castle as she prayed to the God of Creation. *Save me from these vile creatures.* The sweet sound of her voice echoed through the chambers and out the windows of the castle as the nightly reveries continued and the men of the castle grew more and more drunk.

A search of the repulsive bedchamber revealed no weapons for her to use against the wickedness to come. With all the strength she could draw, Judith waited her ill-fate with courage. At the creek of the door, shame pierced her heart at her nakedness as the shadowy form of the barbarian-lord, Holofernes, crossed the threshold. Slamming the door behind him, he crossed to her with great, powerful strides and grabbed her by her hair. Moonlight stretched their shadows into evil-twisted shapes across the vast empty bed.

"They say you are a virgin, girl. Is that true?"

The harshness of his words were like a dagger to Judith's heart. She nearly fainted with the fear. As she was pushed to her knees and rough-handled, she cringed with the pain. Dizzy and fearful of the black glint of lust in the deprived lord's eyes, Judith begged for Holofernes' mercy. The ruthless villain pushed her to the bed, and she closed her eyes to pray for her salvation even as the door slammed open.

Startled, Holofernes and Judith both looked to see a dark form, thick of body and thick of limbs, filling the entry. Knowing naught whether to fear or to praise God, Judith froze while Holofernes, too slowly, reached for the sword at his side. Grendel fully entered the light, a maniac vision with a face twisted with anger, the dark mud dripping with his sweat. Blood dripped from his hands, but Judith did not care how many men he had killed to save her.

Grendel reached the demon King of the Scylding and twisted his neck before he had time to cry out. He tossed the limp body on the bed.

Judith drew back, fear deep in her eyes, and crossed her arms over her naked glory. The fierce giant of a man moved toward her and covered the girl with a loose fur as she pressed herself into the wall. With a gentle motion, he beckoned her to follow.

Judith took a step to follow Grendel out of the despicable room but stopped instead. This had to end, and she could end it. She could not, she would not, spend her life hiding on the moors. The wise girl took Holofernes' sword in her hand. With two strong strokes, she cut off his head and placed it in a bag for proof of what had beset her.

Shocked at Grendel's monstrous path of butchered corpses, Judith followed him back through the castle. He'd done what he'd had to do. He led her to safety through a hidden castle door and stole horses to carry them back to the cave of his mother.

Inside the cave, his mother peeked in the bag. She grinned, the toothless grin of a wicked old woman, and a plan was devised between the three to bring down the Scyldings. If Judith convinced the men of her tribe to battle for their freedom, Grendel would join them. Until then, his life and his part in the rescue of Judith was to remain secret.

Judith returned alone to her city with King Holofernes' head in the sack and claimed to all the people that she had slain the lord as he lay drunk on the bed. Judith's tribe drew courage from the young woman's actions, and she led them into a victorious war, with Grendel helping from the shadows. The tribe took back their land and they honored Judith as their savior.

With their freedom secure, Grendel and his mother returned to the tribe. The new Queen Judith honored them at a grand feast and, with a sparkle in her eye, told the story of Grendel and his lone battles against the enemy on the isolation of the moors. She turned to the man beside her and spoke for everyone to hear. "Your monster from the moors won not only his battles, he has won my heart."

Grendel remained silent although his eyes sparkled with love for his beautiful and brave Queen.

* * *

On the day of their wedding, Grendel stood tall and strong, his scars only adding to the strength of his handsome features. With Judith's hands in his, he spoke the words he'd been unable to say for so long. "I love you, my Queen. You are my heart and my soul and my moon." Their kiss brought rousing cheers from the tribe.

After the ceremony, attendants brought forth Judith's white mare and Grendel's black stallion for their planned ride to the sea. At Judith's request, their night together would be spent in the private cove near Grendel's old cave.

Grendel dismounted first to lift Judith from her horse. She stood in front of him, suddenly shy even as her heart ached for his touch. His kissed her lips gently, as though she might fly away. *This won't do.* This won't do at all. Judith wrapped her arms around his neck and pulled him close for a real kiss. A kiss she'd been wanting for far too long.

As their tongues explored with a new-found freedom, their bodies melted into each other, his hardness firm against her soft belly and his hands on her backside lifting her to her toes as she clung to him. Her white flock and his trousers lay intrusively between them. Judith reached to her shoulder, sliding her fabric to the side, inviting Grendel to taste her skin. Her reaction was immediate, intense, and electrifying as he ran his hand down her shoulder and slipped it inside the bodice to lift her breast and run his thumb across her nipple.

"Judith," he said, placing his mouth to her ear and tickling her with his warm breath. "You are more than a Queen. You are a Goddess."

His husky, seldom heard voice sent goosebumps up her arms and into her belly even as his touch sent hot spasms of lust surging through her. This was the monster of the moors who had killed her enemies and drank their blood. This was the man she desired more than any other. This was the man who would make her a woman. In the light of the setting sun, she stepped back and unfastened her gown, allowing the soft fabric to flow to her feet, and to stand naked before him.

He reached a hand to touch her cheek, his thumb moving delicately along her cheek and chin as though memorizing the contours of her face. He traced the curve of her lips and dipped his mouth to hers. She kissed him, hard, eager, with her hands tangling in his hair, igniting a fire between them. Her body throbbed with desire, and she pushed at his shirt to feel the hardness of his chest and imagine the hardness further down. Her hand reached to his trousers and he groaned, exciting her more as her body took control of her thoughts. The monster was fully awake, and she wanted him to take her.

He dropped to his knees, removing his shirt as he went and dropping his mouth to one breast. His tongue wet her orb and he took it inside, tasting, teasing, and sweeping his tongue along her brown ridges. His free hand moved to her mound and captured her thigh in his grip. As he suckled her breast, drawing it in, releasing, and sucking again, his strong fingers brushed her thigh, up and down, teasing her flesh, heightening her desire, until he rested his thumb on her opening.

"Your skin is so soft," he whispered as his lips moved to her belly and his fingers grasped and curled her female hairs. He gazed at her eyes as his hand reached into the warmth between her thighs and she gasped. She was hot and wet and ready for him and she moaned out her need.

He stood to shed his trousers and she licked her lips at the sight of him naked and fully erect. He grabbed a blanket from his pack and threw it on the sand, and then picked her up and placed her on the blanket, gentle, as if she might break. This was new to Judith, but she spread her legs and beckoned him in, moaning with pleasure when his thickness penetrated her heat. Her fingers gripped and splayed across his back to keep her from floating away. Waves of pleasure pounded into her as he took her as his own. "Grendel, Grendel, Grendel," she shouted out to the darkening sky as her body hit its peak. Their release came together as one and she lay shuddering from the intensity of it just as the moon came out from behind a cloud to flood them with light.

Grendel dropped his weight onto her and buried his face in her hair. "So this is what I've been missing," he said as his fingers ran up and down the outside of her leg.

Her hand stroked at his back. "We are wedded now, which means you can take me whenever you want. However you want. As many times as you want." Her voice playfully carried the tone of a disgruntled wife while inside her body quivered with delight at the thought of it.

Grendel moved off her to lie on his side. His fingers roamed her body, from her hips to her breasts. "Must I?" he asked, as though it would be a chore. He kissed at her neck.

"Yes. It is your royal duty to get me with child. There's to be no getting out of it."

"If you insist." He stood and picked up his naked Queen. His dark eyes turned menacing. "But this time it will be in the monster's den."

Judith drew in her breath as he carried her naked into the darkness of his cave. She wanted no memories of the past to intrude upon her future. Grendel stopped at the edge of the pool and she wondered at the beauty before her. The cave had been cleaned out and transformed into a palace of delight. Candles flickered against the red stone walls and the delightful scent of honeysuckle filled the air. A four-poster bed was set against one wall, and golden goblets and a pitcher sat on a nearby table.

Grendel placed her on the bed, her back resting against the pillows. "I may have slayed the Scyldings, my Queen. But you are the one who slayed the monster of the moors." He bent down on one knee and bowed his head to the floor. "I am your servant from now until forever."

She grabbed a handful of his hair and pulled his head up until he gazed into her eyes.

"No, you are not my servant. You, Grendel, you are my King."

Author Biographies

Julie Behrens lives in Texas with her family and small zoo. She has also published under "Julie Cox." You can learn more about her and her books at www.juliebehrens.com.

Barbra Campbell writes fast and hot contemporary romance/erotic romance as an escape from the regular world. When she was raising her natural born children, exchange students, dogs, cats, birds, horses, chickens, a rabbit, and a cow, she found time to nearly get her PhD in Genetics, help with her husband's construction company, play cello in multiple symphonies, and volunteer for roughly seven hundred organizations. Life happened. New paths were taken, and she's finally escaped most of the rat race to dream up sexy fantasy worlds where the characters are guaranteed a Happily Ever After, or at least a Happy For Now. And since she's busy, she appreciates stories that get right to the point! https://BarbraCampbell.com

Susan Hawes is a self-admitted nerdy girl who works in the medical universe during the day and plays in the online gaming universe at night. The bright side of her children growing up and flying out of the nest is having more time to indulge in her passion for reading and writing. Her additions include cat snuggles, books,

strong coffee, and karaoke. You can find her singing in grocery stores, swinging a big hammer online or on Facebook at
https://www.facebook.com/SusanHawesAuthor/

Alice Kay writes sweet and steamy romance on a mountainside in Colorado. When she's not writing, she enjoys long road trips and driving empty highways late at night. Her quirky characters often find themselves in her favorite settings along the Texas Gulf Coast or the Pacific Northwest. Life without furry friends is unimaginable so her friends and readers may spot a dog or two wandering through her living room and in her books. While much of her writing is contemporary romance and suspense, don't be surprised to find sexy warlocks, powerful love spells, and fire-breathing dragons in upcoming works. Nothing is outside the realm of possibility and no doors are closed to her imagination. You can find her online at www.alicekay.com

Author, coffee lover and self-trained retail therapist, **Rachel Kenley** is the author of seven novels as well as several short stories and novellas. When she is not writing she is homeschooling her sons, trying unsuccessfully to keep up with laundry, and laughing as much as possible. She believes in shameless flirting, never missing the chance to watch *The Wizard of Oz,* and that breakfast can be eaten at any time of day. She is currently the President of the international writers' group Broad Universe and a member of Romance Writers of America. You can follow her on Facebook, Instagram and Twitter and at www.rachelkenley.net

After a mid-life crisis and failing out of college at the age of 20, **Sara Marks** decided to live the life she wanted, not the one expected of her. Now a librarian with two master's degrees, she plans to never stop getting over educated. She started writing as part of the National Novel Writing Month program over 15 years ago. She likes to write women who are like her: feminists who learn to live their life their way; rarely worrying about their age, weight, marriageability, or fertility. They fail and find second, third, and (sometimes) fourth chances to correct their mistakes. Sara's a hopeless romantic who is unlucky in love. She cries at nearly every movie she sees (ask her about when she cried at a horror movie), but it's full-on weeping for Disney animated movies. She loves reading across genres but likes to write women's fiction, romance, and horror. She believes you have to find a balance with the reality of the world if you're going to be a hopeless romantic! You can find more about her works at www.saramarks.net.

M. Reed is the author of several erotic shorts including the Retail Horror series. She holds a B.S. in Biology and an A.A.S. in Mathematics. When she's not writing, she spends her time playing video games, geocaching, and spending time with her husband and dogs.

Trevann Rogers writes rock star romances, urban fantasies, and LGBT paranormal romances. Her books include *House of the Rising Son* and its prequel novella, *After Midnight*. Her stories incorporate an unquenchable addiction to music and her love for vampires, Weres, incubi and rock stars. Trevann writes long after the sun goes down because like these elusive creatures, she learned long ago that sometimes being yourself means Living After Midnight. Trevann lives in Connecticut with Molly, Chloe and Toby, three rescue mutts, and Lil Monkey, a sock monkey who thinks he's real. You can find her online at: www.trevannrogers.com and www.facebook.com/trevannr

Divya Sood is the author of three novels the latest being *Find Someone to Love* (Riverdale Avenue Books, 2019). She studied Creative Writing and English at Rutgers University. While at Rutgers, she was awarded the NJ Chapter of Arts and Letters First Prize for Fiction, the Edna N. Herzberg First Prize for Fiction, and the Edith Hamilton First Prize for Fiction. She pursued graduate work and earned a Master of Arts in English from New York University (NYU). She has attended the Breadloaf Writers Conference. She has been published in *The Masters Review Anthology VIII.* She currently teaches at Gotham Writers Workshop in New York City, NY and is an adjunct professor of Creative Writing at Southern New Hampshire University (SNHU). Website: www.div.nyc

Other Riverdale Avenue Titles You Might Enjoy

Dangerous Curves
Edited by Rachel Kenley

Women Who Love Monsters
Edited by Lori Perkins

Gone with the Dead: An Anthology of Romance and Horror
Edited by Lori Perkins

Amorous Congress
Edited by F. Leonora Solomon

The Circlet Treasury of Steampunk Erotica
Edited by Cecelia Tan

www.ingramcontent.com/pod-product-compliance
Lightning Source LLC
Chambersburg PA
CBHW071432260626
47170CB00008B/2690